Heavenly Praise for
Breakfasts with *Archangel Shecky*

"I've found many lost items for my good friend, Archangel
Shecky. When you drink as much scotch as Shecky does, you tend
to lose things more frequently. One thing Shecky has never lost,
though, is his sense of humor. It comes across in this book.**"**

> —St. Anthony of Padua, author of the jingle, "St. Anthony,
> St. Anthony, please come down. Something's lost and
> must be found."

"I've worked with a lot of hopeless cases in my career. Archangel
Shecky has always been one of my favorites. His wisdom can help
many people who feel their careers are hopeless.**"**

> —St. Jude, Patron of Lost Causes

"Killing dragons is rather easy once you get the hang of it.
Killing some of the myths and fears people have about succeeding
is much more difficult. My good buddy, Archangel Shecky, does
a masterful job of it.**"**

> —St. George, Dragon Slayer

"Legend has it that I helped people get from one side of a
treacherous river to the other. The 'tips' that Archangel Shecky has
written on napkins in this book can help anybody who reads and
applies them get from where they are now in their lives to where
they want to be. That's a nice road to travel.**"**

> —St. Christopher, Patron Saint of Travelers

"Do as he says; not as he does. Archangel Shecky is very good at
handing out wonderfully worthwhile advice. He's not always so good
at following it.**"**

> —Shecky's own Guardian Angel (name withheld by request)

To Mel & Sharon,
Keep on laughing
Best Always
Gene Perret

Breakfasts with
Archangel Shecky

And His Infallible, Irrefutable, Unassailable,
One-Size-Fits-All Secrets of Success

by Gene Perret

Quill
Driver
Books

Fresno, California

Printed in the United States of America.

Published by
Quill Driver Books, Inc.
an imprint of Linden Publishing
2006 South Mary, Fresno, CA, 93721
559-233-6633/800-345-4447
QuillDriverBooks.com

Quill Driver Books books may be purchased for educational,
fund-raising, business or promotional use. Please contact
Special Markets, Quill Driver Books Inc., at the above address
or phone numbers.

Quill Driver Books Project Cadre:
Christine Hernandez, Maura J. Zimmer,
Stephen Blake Mettee, Kent Sorsky

135798642

ISBN 1-884956-92-0 • 978-1884956-92-8

To order a copy of this book, please call
1-800-345-4447.

Library of Congress Cataloging-in-Publication Data

Perret, Gene.
  Breakfasts with Archangel Shecky : and his infallible,
irrefutable, unassailable, one-size-fits-all secrets of success /
by Gene Perret.
     p. cm.
  ISBN-13: 978-1-884956-92-8
  ISBN-10: 1-884956-92-0
  1. Comedians--Fiction 2. Guardian angels--Fiction.
 3. Philadelphia (Pa.)--Fiction. I. Title.
  PS3616.E7656B74 2008
  813'.6--dc22
                            2008040387

Many guardian angels have graced my life and career.
This book is my tribute to each of you.

CHAPTER ONE...

SOMETIMES IT'S HARD TO SEE THE AUDIENCE IN THE GLARE of the spotlight, but it's exhilarating to know they're out there. When they acknowledge your humor with an explosion of laughter or enthusiastic applause, it's captivating, intoxicating, spellbinding.

I've been under comedy's spell for most of my life, but especially since I got out of high school and worked up the courage to face an open-mike audience and give standup a try.

You may have heard of me, I'm Chuck Barry. At the age of 24, I was a not-so-famous Philadelphia truck driver and wannabe legendary stand-up comedian on the verge of completely abandoning the comedy gig and concentrating all my energies on remaining a not-so-famous, lackluster, go-nowhere Philadelphia truck driver. That's how demoralized I was feeling at the time.

Background information? I've been single my whole life. Born and raised in Philadelphia. The nuns taught me from Kindergarten through 8th grade. The priests taught me through four years of high school. Nobody taught me in college because I didn't go.

Right after high school I landed a job for a wholesale company in the neighborhood driving a truck that delivers candy, cigarettes, and stuff like that to small drug stores around town. It was a terrible job with terrible pay and no chance for advancement. I sat in the front of the truck already, and that's as far as I was ever going to get with that outfit. But I took the crummy, dead-end job because it allowed me to devote my weekends and energy to my real career goal—standup.

My parents were upset that I didn't go to college, but a degree in whatever wouldn't have helped me because I had other plans. I was going to thrill the world with my comedy genius. Oh, my beginning would be unspectacular—a few open-mike appearances just to sharpen my skills and learn to feel at ease with an audience. Then people would notice. They'd show up for my performances at local clubs prompting more gigs and higher pay. I'd travel the national comedy club circuit for awhile, like Seinfeld and Romano. Eventually, I'd make it in television and be rich, famous, and exorbitantly happy—like Seinfeld and Romano and Drew Carey and Gary Shandling and all those other rich, famous, and happy guys.

That's what I thought.

That's not what happened. For six years I struggled to get stage time at the open-mike nights. Those, of course, don't pay anything. A few of the clubs in Philadelphia and the surrounding areas would hire me for small money, but I wasn't making much career progress. I most certainly wasn't in the "rich, famous, and exorbitantly happy" department.

Sure, every so often I would hear that explosion of laughter and appreciative applause that sends a thrill all though you, but over those six years my glorious hopes gradually dissolved into disillusionment and despair. My dad was threatening to toss me out of the house if I didn't start looking for a "real" job. He was convinced that driving a truck for the kind of money I made wasn't a real job and, to him, being a stand-up comedian was a euphemism for "no good, lazy, bum." If he tossed me out, it wouldn't have made me lazy and no good, but it would have made me a bum. I couldn't afford to get a place of my own on my crummy salary.

I'd been dating a girl who was pretty good at keeping my spirits up when I got down, but she was trying to end our relationship. At least that's the impression I got when I received an invitation to her wedding. I didn't blame her, though. She didn't necessarily want someone who was rich, famous, and exorbitantly happy, but she apparently wanted someone—and deserved someone—with at least a promise of a future. I didn't have that.

It didn't look like I ever would have that.

One dark night my set at the Laff House hadn't gone so well. Actually, it was terrible. The crowd didn't laugh or even chuckle much. They didn't even think I was good enough to heckle. There was no applause at all, except when I left the stage.

So there I was, sitting at the bar in the back of the club sipping a scotch, feeling sorry for myself, and wondering if I wouldn't have done better listening to my mother's advice that I should become a doctor or a dentist or even a candlestick maker. My father's constant warm paternal offering, "Get the hell off your keester and get a decent job," swirled through my head.

I sat alone and drank and thought about my future. Normally when I played this club or stopped in to hear the other comedians, Frank, the bartender, and I would solve all the problems of the Phillies or the Eagles or the

Flyers, but Frank was busy washing and drying glasses. Actually, Frank was pretending to be busy washing and drying glasses because he wanted to avoid talking to me. When you bomb at a comedy club, all the people who work there and the other comics avoid you for two reasons—first, they know you would prefer to suffer in silence, and second they would rather not be seen hanging out with a loser.

So my scotch and my self-sympathy were my only companions. Then a man sat at the empty barstool next to mine and began a friendly conversation with, "You were lousy tonight."

I turned, expecting to confront some wise-cracking punk who couldn't work up the courage to heckle me while I was onstage, but now wanted to impress his date by hurling a few insults—and maybe a few punches—at the not-so-funny comedian. Instead I was looking at an innocent, frail, old man (of course, to me, at the ripe age of 24, everyone over 35 was old). He wore tattered, grubby clothes. Nothing he had on matched anything else he had on.

I decided he wasn't looking for a fight. He was apparently just a panhandler who wasn't doing so well on the streets so he came inside trying to bum a couple of bucks off some generous drunks.

I was a little disappointed that he wasn't looking for a fight because I was in the mood to beat the crap out of someone. It would have taken my mind off the beating up I was giving myself for putting on such a lousy act earlier. If I beat the crap out of this little guy, it might have improved my state of mind, but I would have felt bad about it afterwards.

Still, he insulted me and my act so I had to say something sharp and incisive in my own defense. I said, "What did you say?" Okay, it was neither sharp nor incisive but it's the standard delaying tactic I used when I needed time to think of a clever retort.

"You were lousy tonight," he repeated without hesitation.

Now I was tempted to beat the crap out of him even if it did mean I would feel terrible about it afterwards.

"What?" I asked. "Do you know everything about comedy?"

He said, "No, I don't know everything about comedy."

I sipped my scotch on the rocks just long enough to give him a superior glance and said, "Then keep your stupid opinions to yourself."

He said, "But I do know a little bit about comedy."

"Oh yeah? Well, what exactly do you know?" I cleverly retorted.

"I know if you go up onstage and do eighteen minutes and you get two, maybe three chuckles, then you were lousy."

There was probably no point in me, an almost professional comic, trying to talk sense to a civilian, but I felt I had to defend myself and my act against this idiot. I said, "Some of that stuff I did tonight kills. This was just a bad audience. You should have seen me last weekend when I played the Comedy Cabaret."

"Oh, I see," he said. "Some nights you're great and then other nights you're not so hot."

"That's right. That's the way show business goes."

"So do you think Frank Sinatra was like that? Do you think he came out for a show and said, 'Ladies and gentlemen, I'm not so hot tonight, but you should have seen me last Thursday. I was terrific. It's a shame you couldn't have been there then, but thanks for spending a fortune to come see the show tonight. Do come back again, though, and who knows, maybe next time you'll catch me on a good night.'"

I took a good long sip of my scotch to give this clown time to realize what a stupid statement he just made. Finally I replied, "No, I don't think the great Frank Sinatra ever did that."

"Do you want to know what I think?"

This bum was starting to annoy me. My response was probably louder than it should have been, "You know, pal, I don't really care what you think. You told me I was lousy tonight. You got that off your chest. Now why don't you just move along and leave me the hell alone?"

Frank stopped pretending he was cleaning glasses and started towards us. When he saw there was no real threat of an altercation—it was just me and an old bum—he went back to polishing glasses. Anything to keep from hanging out near a loser like me, I guessed.

My rant did nothing to deter this pest. "What are you getting so sore at?" he asked. "I'm not telling you anything you don't know. You can't accomplish anything worthwhile by being hit and miss—good on Monday, hot on Tuesday, lousy on Friday. You have to be steadfast—a professional every time you walk on stage."

There was no point in telling this clown that I'd just about made up my mind that I would never step on a stage again. Instead I went on the defense. "Nobody can be top-notch every time. Everyone has an off night."

"Maybe so," he replied, "but the pro finds out why he was off and fixes it the next time out."

"So maybe I'll be great the next time."

"Maybe don't feed the bulldog."

I had no idea what that meant and I didn't really care. "Yeah, well, why don't you go home and feed your bulldog and leave me alone?"

He stared at me for a moment then said, "C'mon, lighten up. Buy me a drink."

"Why? Give me one good reason why I should buy you a drink?"

"Because I cared enough to tell you that you were lousy tonight." He called to Frank. "Bartender, I'll have whatever he's having. What is it?"

Frank said, "Scotch on the rocks."

"Yeah, I'll have that. Give me scotch on the rocks."

Frank seemed to sense that this guy was a deadbeat, so he glanced at me and my nod signaled that it was okay to put it on my tab. Maybe a sip of the spirits would soften his mood and he'd be less insulting.

Frank poured the drink and set it in front of the bum, pulled a couple of bills out from under my glass, and rang it up on the register. The blockhead picked up his glass, sipped the scotch, sighed, and said, "This stuff is pretty damned good."

I said, "What? Like you've never had scotch before?"

"No," he said, "I never have. I'm not from around here."

"What the hell does that have to do with anything? This is not a local drink. Scotch is all over."

"Really? Like where?"

"Like Scotland for one."

He sipped a little more. "This stuff is really good."

I said, "If you're not from around here, where abouts are you from?"

"Heaven."

I laughed at that. "Heaven? Where in the hell is Heaven?"

"That's very funny."

"What?"

"What you just said."

"What did I just say?"

"You said, 'Where in the hell is Heaven?' Heaven can't be in Hell because they're two opposite places."

"It was just a figure of speech."

"Yeah, but it was funny. It was funnier than anything that was in your act."

"Yeah, I know...I was lousy tonight." I figured, if you can't beat 'em, join 'em.

"So where is Heaven really?" I asked. "Arkansas? Georgia? You know we have a place right here in Pennsylvania called Paradise."

"Heaven isn't anyplace. It just is."

"What do you mean, it just is?"

"It just is—with God and the saints and the angels and all."

"You better take it easy with the scotch, old timer." I held up my glass to cue Frank that I wanted a refill.

The old man caught my signal and held up his glass. "Yeah, me too. This stuff is pretty damned good."

Frank brought two more and lifted a few more bills of mine from the bar. I decided to play along with this clown, whatever his game. I said, "So you live with the saints and the angels and like that?"

"Yeah."

"Do you live there all the time or like just for a couple of days after your social security check comes?"

He sipped his scotch and said, "No, all the time."

I asked, "What do you do in Heaven?"

He said, "I'm a guardian angel."

I had to laugh at that. "A guardian angel?"

In school the nuns taught us kids that we all had a special guardian angel who was to watch over us and protect us from evil and harm. "Oh, you'll never see him," the good Sisters would tell us, "but he's with you every minute of every day and every night." The nuns never mentioned to us youngsters that our guardian angel might come into a club one night and con us into buying him a couple of drinks.

Still chuckling, I said, "You don't dress like a guardian angel."

"And all the other guardian angels you've met in your life, how did they dress?"

I shrugged. "I guess you've got me there."

"Look, a guardian angel's job—my job—is to hang around and protect you folks." He paused long enough to take a generous sip of his scotch. "And God knows, literally, that most of you people are nitwits. So we have a tough job. Do you think that wearing a long white robe with sissy little angel wings shooting out of our shoulder blades and carrying a harp around would make this job any easier?"

"I never thought of it."

"Most of you people don't think of anything anyway. That's why you need guardian angels."

Gene Perret

"So who do you protect?" I asked

"You. I'm your guardian angel."

"You're my guardian angel?"

He said, "Right."

This little guy was starting to amuse me. He was a certified nut, but he was taking my mind off the bad show I had just done. I held out my hand and said, "Well, it's nice to meet you after all these years. I'm Chuck Barry."

He shook my hand vigorously and said, "I know that. Don't you think after being your guardian angel for twenty-five years I would know your name?"

He tripped himself up with that statement and I called him on it. I said, "You must be one incompetent guardian angel. I'm only twenty-four years old so you couldn't have been guarding me for twenty-five years."

He said, "No, you're really twenty-five years old. Your mother lied to you. You were born before she was married."

"What the hell are you saying...."

"Relax, take it easy," he said. "I'm kidding you. It's a joke...a little archangel humor. You think you're the only one who can do bad jokes tonight?"

I laughed a bit at that, but reluctantly. "So, what's your name?"

"I'm a guardian angel. I specialize in show business folks, especially comedy. I'm the Archangel Shecky."

I said, "C'mon...you're kidding."

He said, "Of course, I'm kidding. Not even God would be that hokey. You can call me Bill."

I decided that maybe I could have a bit more fun with him. "So tell me, Bill, do you know all the saints and all?"

He answered as if I had asked a serious question. "I know all the saints. That's why I can help you; I've got contacts. I know Matthew, Mark, Luke, and John—all pretty good writers."

"Yeah," I added. "I understand they have a best-seller out."

He ignored my sarcasm. "I know St. Francis—both Xavier and Assisi. I know Saints Xanthippe and Polyxene the Righteous. We have a lot of laughs up there kidding them about those names. Old Polyxene's not so righteous when I get on a roll about his name, I'll tell you that. St. Anthony, the patron saint of lost things, is a good friend of mine. You lose something, you come to me, I go to him— Bam!—you got it back."

"Can you find me an agent?"

"That I can't do. I don't have any contacts there. Agents don't have guardian angels."

"Well then thanks for nothing."

"But I can help you get yourself an agent, better paying gigs, and pretty much anything else you want."

"Well, don't put yourself out," I said. "I'm about to give up this whole show business dream anyway."

"You don't have to you know. You can get what you want."

"Look, I've been trying to get what I want for six years and it hasn't happened."

"Oh, that settles it then, because six years is the limit. If you don't get it after that, there's no use trying anymore. You're absolutely right to quit."

"Well, then, maybe that's just what I'll do," I said sounding like a pouty little girl.

"Why? Because you were lousy tonight?'

I raised my voice a little too much again. "Yeah, that's part of it—because I was lousy tonight. I was terrible. I stunk up the place. I'm no good at this."

He held up his hand to calm me. "Hey, there's nothing wrong with being lousy."

"Oh, that's a brilliant statement—'There's nothing wrong with being lousy.'"

"You know years ago, probably before you remember, people had television sets with rabbit ears that you had to move all over the place to get a picture. There was no color; it was all black and white. You only got three channels, and the picture would get all squiggly and fuzzy and snowy. They were lousy television sets."

"And you're saying there's nothing wrong with that."

"No, because those sets led to color television. They led to the big screens you have today with the high definition and the TiVo and all that other fancy stuff. Lousy is necessary to get to good, and good is what you have to go through to get to great."

With that proclamation he took a self-satisfied gulp of scotch. I just looked at him, bewildered.

"What the hell are you talking about?" I said.

He said, "Let me spell it out for you." He grabbed one of the cocktail napkins that was on the bar, took out a felt-tip marker, and began writing something on it. When he finished he made a big show of putting the cap back on the pen and clipping it into his pocket, then he gave me the napkin and said, "Read this and think about it before you do anything hasty."

I glanced at the napkin. On it he had written:

If you want to be great, start with lousy

For some reason an angry flush crept up my back. "Who are you to say whether I'm lousy or not?" I asked, forgetting I'd admitted I was lousy just a few minutes before. "Besides, what's it to you? Why do you care whether I get what I want or not?"

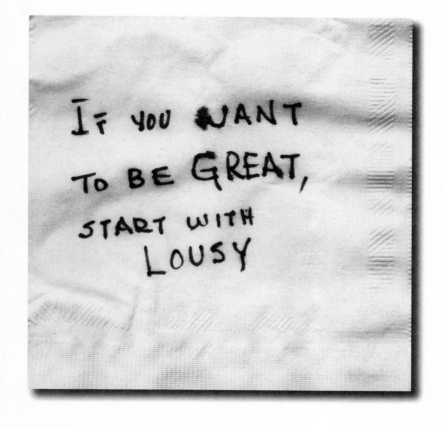

"Because you deserve it?"

"Oh, really? Why do I deserve it more than anyone else?"

"You don't tell jokes real good and you don't listen real good, either."

He grabbed another cocktail napkin. "I'm going to write this out for you, too. I didn't say you deserve it more than anyone else. I said you deserve it." With a flourish he held up the napkin. In big letters it read:

You deserve whatever it is you want

I said, "That's quite a statement. But how do you know I deserve what I want?"

"Everyone does—you, the other comedians, anybody who has a goal deserves to reach it."

"There's all that success to go around, huh?"

"When you take a breath of air, do you worry that you're stealing it from someone else? No. There's enough for all. There are enough achievements in this world for anyone who has a dream."

"And now you, as my guardian angel, are going to teach me how to do that."

"Right. In fact, I've already started."

"You did? That's funny, I didn't notice."

"Why doesn't that surprise me? You didn't notice because you were too busy being negative. You're so convinced that it's not going to happen—that it can't happen to you—that you haven't heard anything I've taught you."

"Refresh my memory."

"Reread the napkins. I taught you that you're entitled to get whatever you want, that you deserve it, and that it is your

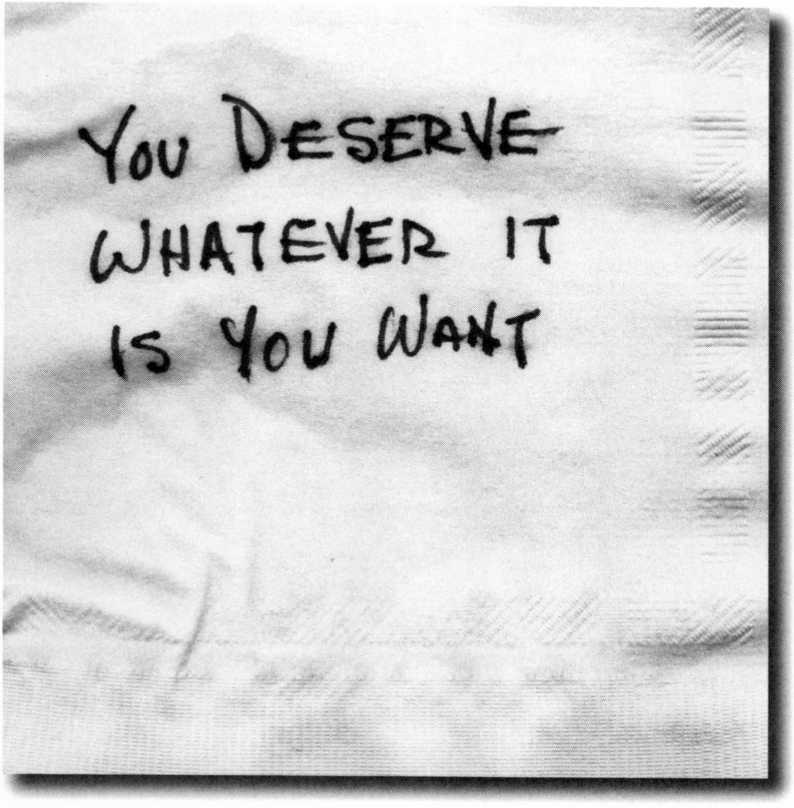
YOU DESERVE
WHATEVER IT
IS YOU WANT

absolute right to go after it. You can't run from opportunity when it knocks because you feel you're unworthy of it."

"So if I buy into that nonsense, we can go on to lesson two, right?"

"Actually, that was lesson two."

"What happened to lesson one?"

"I don't know why I write these things out if you're going to ignore them. Read the first napkin I gave you."

I retrieved the cocktail napkin and read aloud, "If you want to be Great, start with Lousy."

"That's right, and we'll talk more about that later."

"I don't think there's going to be a later." That was enough pap for me for one night. Gathering my change from the bar and leaving a fairly generous tip for Frank—even though he wanted nothing to do with me all night—I said, "Look, ...uh...." I was trying to remember his name.

He reminded me, "Bill."

"Look, Bill, I've almost enjoyed talking with you. You took my mind off the terrible performance I gave tonight."

He said, "Yeah you were lousy."

Bill grabbed me by the arm as I began to leave and said, "You don't believe I'm real, do you?"

I said, "Bill, my friend, I certainly believe you're real. I believe you're a real flako. I believe your elevator doesn't go to the top floor. I believe the right side of your brain doesn't quite know where the left side of your brain went when it retired."

He said, "If you had lines like that in your act, you might have gotten a few laughs tonight."

"Yeah, yeah, I know...I was lousy tonight. But no, Bill, I don't believe you're a real guardian angel."

He challenged me. "Why not?"

"Look, Bill, I really have to get home, but, okay, let me ask you a question. Do you believe that a leprechaun can really lead you to a pot of gold at the end of a rainbow? Do you believe that the Tooth Fairy would actually leave good money for a useless molar? Do you believe if you kiss a frog it might turn into a gorgeous prince? Then why should I believe that a bum off the street who's doing nothing more than trying to scam a few drinks out of me would be my blessed, sacred guardian angel?"

Bill said, "That's actually four questions, but let me respond by asking you, an aspiring Philadelphia comedian, one question. What the hell is a toasted sticky bun?"

CHAPTER TWO...

DON'T ASK ME HOW OR WHY, BUT I WOUND UP TAKING MY new friend and alleged guardian angel, at 1 o'clock in the morning, to the Melrose Diner for a toasted sticky bun and a cup of coffee.

Bill loved the sticky bun.

"I gotta tell you...these things are pretty damned delicious."

"You mean to tell me you've never had a sticky bun before?" I asked.

"No. I told you...I'm not from around here."

"Yeah, I know. You're from Heaven. You live with the angels and saints and all that baloney."

"Right."

I said, "You know, most of the time after I do a bad show I go home and I can't sleep. Tonight, I'm going to sleep like a baby."

Bill said, "Because I took your mind off your lousy show?"

I answered, "No. Because you're boring me to death with this angel fraud of yours."

Bill seemed offended. "You still don't believe me?"

"So far, you've gotten two drinks out of me and I'm sure I'm going to have to pick up the tab here, so I believe that you're pulling a fast one. And I'm falling for it."

Bill said, "I'll pay you back for the drinks if you want and I'll pay my share of this check. We angels get a per diem, you know."

I said, "Boy, you don't give up, do you?"

"Guardian angels aren't supposed to give up. And we're not supposed to let you give up, either."

It seemed useless to try to shake this character from his imbecilic angel fantasy. I said, "Okay, you got me to come here for a bite to eat and a cup of coffee because you said you wanted to talk to me. So what shall we talk about?"

"You . . . your comedy . . .your life."

I said, "I know. You think I'm lousy."

"I also told you that there's nothing wrong with being lousy. There's only something wrong with staying lousy. Besides, I don't think you're lousy; I think your act is lousy."

"Oh, like there's a difference."

"There's a big difference. Let me tell you a story...."

Before he began the story, though, he took another big bite of cinnamon bun and chewed on it for a bit. He was trying to chew a bit faster so he could get to his message, but it wasn't working. Finally he swallowed and said, "These things are really pretty damned good, you know that?"

I said, "You were going to tell me a story?"

"Oh yeah, one time Phyllis Diller. You've heard of Phyllis Diller, haven't you?"

"Yeah, I heard of her."

"Well . . ." He took another mouthful and chewed for awhile. "Delicious. Well, one night a long time ago, when she was just starting out, she was working in a small club and Bob Hope was in the audience. You've heard of Bob Hope, right?"

"Yeah, I think. Didn't he play first base for the Yankees?"

"No, he was a famous comedian...."

I said, "I know who Bob Hope was, for crying out loud." This guy was going to teach me about comedy and he couldn't even recognize when I was doing a joke.

He went on. "Well, Hope was Phyllis Diller's idol. She studied his style, his joke forms, she wanted to be just like him. Only she wasn't yet. And this night her act bombed. She was awful. You may know the feeling."

"Just tell me the stupid story, okay?"

"Okay. Well, Phyllis was so embarrassed that even though she would love to meet Bob Hope, she tried to sneak out of the theatre without seeing him. She was that bad. But Hope caught up with her. She said, 'Mr. Hope, I'm so embarrassed by my show tonight. You must think I'm terrible.' Hope said, 'Honey, I think you're terrific. You've got it. Stick with it.'"

Well, Phyllis was so encouraged by his faith in her talent that she went on to become a legend in comedy. What do you think of that?"

I said, "You live with God, the angels, and the saints, and now you're going to tell me you know Phyllis Diller and Bob Hope personally?"

"I'm telling you a story," he said, sounding miffed. "What the hell difference does it make whether I know the people personally or not?"

"I didn't know angels were allowed to curse this much."

"Hell is not a curse. It's a foreign country. But see, that's why my job is so tough. You're missing the whole point of the story. Your guardian angel is telling you something that is going to help you and you don't even listen."

I'd had about enough. "Will you get off the angel bit? The routine is starting to get a little tired."

"Well, you would certainly know about that."

"That's getting a little tired, too—you're constantly insulting me."

"I'm not insulting you. I'm telling you the truth."

I slammed my coffee cup down splashing lukewarm coffee all over the table. Bill quickly pulled what was left of his precious sticky bun out of harm's way. Fearing any further jeopardy, he forked the last chunk into his mouth and chewed....well...he chewed ecstatically.

I said, "Then tell me the truth. Tell me you're Bill from Oshkosh, Minnesota, or..."

He said, "Oshkosh is in Wisconson." Then added almost under his breath, "These people are nitwits."

I ignored him. It didn't matter where Oshkosh was. "...or you're from Sri Lanka or you're from Oxnard, California. Tell me the truth and stop telling me you're my guardian angel."

He took a sip of coffee, probably to give me a few seconds to calm down. Then he said...no...he proclaimed, "Look, I don't need your approval to do my job. And I certainly don't need your belief. As I said, most of you people are nitwits. Most of you are too dumb to believe in guardian angels. That's okay. I still gotta do what I gotta do."

Now it was my turn to sip some coffee, but my cup was empty. The waitress came over to clean up the mess I had made. She wasn't happy about it, but what else did she have to do? We were the only two people in the place—my guardian angel and I.

The fresh coffee she poured for me smelled delicious, so I tasted it and said, "Okay, prove to me that you're an angel." I shoved my coffee cup towards him. "Turn this into wine."

He shoved the cup back. "You've had enough to drink tonight."

I had him cornered. "You can't do it, can you?"

He said, "No, I can't. We don't work that way."

I said, "That's bull."

He said, "We're not authorized to do miracles just to entertain."

I felt I had him cornered again. "It wouldn't be entertainment. If you're an angel, it would prove to me that you really are an angel."

He said, "It would prove nothing. Jesus worked miracles and look where it got Him."

I wouldn't surrender. "You're copping out, Bill. You're not an angel and you can't do angel things."

He said, "You're copping out. You don't believe in angels and yet you know what things they can and can't do?"

I reached for the check and started to get up. "I gotta go."

Bill put his hand on mine and said, "I got the bill. Sit down."

As I said earlier, I don't know how or why I came to this diner with this clown in the first place and I don't know why I sat down when he said to. Maybe he was casting some sort of supernatural spell over me.

Bill said, "Look, you're an intelligent guy...."

I said, "I thought we were all nitwits."

"You're one of the more intelligent nitwits."

"Thank you...I think."

"Look, you wanted proof that I'm an angel. I'm sorry I can't do the coffee into wine bit, but I have another proposition."

"Uh-oh, that settles it. Here comes the money part of your con."

"This will cost you nothing but a little bit of your time. Are you interested?"

"No."

"You care about your comedy and you want to make it in the business. I can help you do that."

"Oh, you, a glorified panhandler who is bumming drinks and a meal, are going to teach me, a hit and miss local comedian, how to be a success?"

"I don't have to teach you that. You already know how to be a success."

"I'm a success?" I asked. "Me? I'm a low-paid delivery boy who does comedy that sometimes gets laughs and sometimes doesn't. You say I'm a success?"

He said, "You sure don't listen real good." He took a fresh napkin from the dispenser on the table and uncapped the felt-tip pen again.

When he was finished writing, he said, "I didn't say you were a success. I said . . ." and he held the napkin up in front of my face:

You already know how to be a success

He dealt the napkin across the table at me as if it were a playing card. It made a complete revolution and stopped so the words were facing me. I had to laugh at the stupidity

YOU ALREADY
KNOW HOW TO
BE A SUCCESS

of it. I said, "Well if I do know it, I certainly don't know I know it."

Bill said, "You're a truck driver, right?"

"No, I pilot the Space Shuttle."

My sarcasm didn't deter him. "To be a truck driver, you have to know how to drive, right?"

"Boy, you angels are smart people."

"We're not people, but we are smart. And thank you for the compliment," he said, matching my sarcasm. "You weren't born knowing how to drive a truck, were you?"

"What are you getting at?"

"When you get to where you're delivering stuff, how do you get from your truck to the store?"

"I get out of my truck and I walk there."

"You walk." He said it in a way that sounded as if he were amazed at that. "You weren't born knowing how to walk, were you?"

"Of course not."

"You had to struggle to learn to walk. I'll bet you fell on your cute little bottom quite a few times."

"All kids do. That's how they learn."

"Exactly. But they get up again and keep doing it until they're walking. And do you know why?"

"I'm sure you're going to tell me."

"Because they want to. They have a desire to learn to walk. So they do."

"So I'm a successful walker. Wonderful."

"Was it difficult for you to learn to drive?"

"No, anybody can learn how to drive."

"Exactly. You knew you could do it, so you did."

"What does that prove?"

Bill poked his finger on the table top for emphasis. "It proves you succeeded at least twice in your life. It proves that if you want something badly enough and you honestly believe—no, you honestly know you can get it—you'll get it."

To me this whole concept seemed silly. I said, "You're making some pretty grand assumptions from some fairly simple events."

He said, "That's exactly what I'm trying to tell you. You can learn to achieve bigger things simply by recalling how you achieved the smaller things. You already know how to achieve what you want, but you won't admit it to yourself."

"Learning to walk and to drive are a lot different from making it in show business."

"Are they? Would you be willing to try a little experiment with me? It'll help your act."

Somehow I was allowing this fraud to raise my curiosity. I said, "Why not? I'm apparently not going to get any sleep tonight anyway. Shoot."

He said, "You do a bit in your act about you and your father and the relationship between the two of you."

"Yeah?"

He said, "You do some pretty good lines in there."

"That's quite an improvement over 'You were lousy tonight.'"

"You were, but there were some pretty good lines. You do one about how your father wanted you to play football for Penn State."

"Yeah. I say: I just missed playing tackle for Penn State. I just missed by about 186 pounds."

"That's good. Then you talk about how your father thinks he's an athlete."

"Right. I say: He tries to stay in shape by playing golf.
Do you believe that? The exercise value of playing golf is
roughly equivalent to . . . being in a coma."

"Yeah, that played nice."

"Then I add: . . . except in a coma, you can't cheat."

"Funny."

"Well, thanks."

"Then it goes nowhere."

"I guess I said 'thanks' too soon."

"No, I don't mean that in a bad way. You've got a good
routine going, but it just stops. You talk about how bad a
golfer your dad is, then you just abandon that and move
on to another topic."

"Well, I can't talk about what a lousy golfer he is
forever."

"I know that, but you have to end the routine. Otherwise it feels unfinished—like you just threw it in there. You
need a strong joke to finish."

"So, do you have one?"

He said, "No. You do."

"I do?"

"Yeah. Here's my proposition. Here's my test, my proof,
as you call it. I want you to spend the whole week just
thinking about one joke. Not a new routine; just one great
joke. A joke that will finish off that chunk of material."

I asked, "You want one joke?"

He said, "No. I want one great joke."

I said, "How do I know when I've got a..." I emphasized
the word in a way of mocking him, I suppose. "...great joke?"

"You'll know. Don't work on anything else and don't
stop until you get it. Will you do that?"

"No," I said and stood up to end the discussion.

"No?" he said with great indignity. "How can you say 'no' to your guardian angel?"

"I do it like this," I said. Then I repeated the word with dramatic emphasis to show him that I really meant it.

"Do you know the penalty for saying 'no' to a guardian angel?"

"No. What is the penalty for saying 'no' to a guardian angel?"

"You have to pick up the check for this meal." He held the check out to me.

I grabbed the check from his hand. "Big deal," I said. "You were going to stick me with this tab no matter what I said."

I started to leave, then turned to him again. I said, "If you are my guardian angel—and I'm certainly not saying you are—but if you are, shouldn't you just be keeping me from getting hit by a car, falling out of a tree, or having a safe crash down on my head? Why are you interested in my act?"

He said, "Sometimes we like to adlib."

I shook my head at the absurdity of this man.

He said, "Do the experiment."

"Why should I? Why should I bust my hump for one line when I'm fed up to here with comedy? I'm getting out of the business and I'm not writing anymore lines—good, great, or stinko."

I started for the door. He shouted after me, "You'll do it! Once I put that idea in your head, you can't not do it!"

When I reached the door and pushed it open, he shouted, "Just one great line!" I went out without looking back, determined not to do his stupid experiment. I was done trying to be a stand-up comedian.

CHAPTER THREE...

BILL, MY GUARDIAN ANGEL, WAS RIGHT—AS MUCH AS I HATE TO admit that. The challenge he planted in my mind remained there, taunting me to write that one great line. Different lines kept popping into my head all week. Some were pretty good so I toyed with them and tried to make them great. Rewording made some of the gags better; it made some of them worse. It didn't make any of them great.

Then an idea popped into my head, like a miracle. Whoops...I should have used a different word there. It sounds like I was starting to believe in this angel malarkey. Let's say it was inspiration, rather than a miracle. Many comedy writers say that the great jokes are all floating out there in the ether and all we have to do is pluck them out of the air.

Well, that's kind of the way I got this line—plucked it from somewhere. I don't know where. I played with it, polished it, refined it. I tried saying it one way and then another and finally came up with the line I was going to deliver.

It was the Saturday night after the guardian angel visitation and I was filling in for a guy who didn't show at the Comedy Cabaret in Northeast Philly. The act was going over okay. Scattered laughs. Better than the previous Sunday's gig. I wasn't bombing but I wasn't exactly making them choke on their drinks with laughter, either.

The "athlete-golf" routine, though, was playing nicely. Maybe a lot of people in the audience had dads who mistakenly thought they were athletes, too. Who knows. But I came to the line.

I stepped forward when I was going to deliver it because I kind of felt instinctively that it was special. I told the audience, "I'll give you an idea how bad a golfer my dad really is. He never rents a cart when he plays. Where he hits the ball, it's cheaper to take public transportation."

Bam! The audience bought it. They screamed. Giant laughs. And then, get this—applause. Applause!

I didn't really care how the rest of the act went. That one joke worked and that made me feel pretty good.

After my set, I sat at the bar and Dan, the bartender there, even spoke to me. He said, "That golf joke about your dad was funny. The rest of your set sucked." So much for feeling pretty good.

As I was sinking back into my comedy-career despair, my "guardian angel" sat down beside me and said, "Scotch, please."

Dan served the drink. The only money on the bar was mine. Dan gave a signal that said, "What should I do?" I pointed to my cash and Dan took the price of the drink from it.

Bill raised his glass in a gesture of thanks and said, "You were less lousy tonight."

I said, "That's a big compliment coming from you."

"Yes, it is."

"How did you know where I was playing tonight? How did you find me?"

"I told you. One of my closest friends is St. Anthony. He can find anything."

"Oh, that's right. You've got pals in Heaven."

"Everybody does. You, above all, should know that by now."

"Why should I know it above everybody else?"

He said, "That line played gangbusters tonight."

"Which line?"

"You know which line. C'mon, don't play dumb with me. Oh, that's right. I forgot—when you play dumb, you're not really playing."

I said, "Why are you always insulting me?"

"You know me. I'm a very unlikable angel."

"You sure are. You must turn Heaven into a regular Hell."

"Okay, I'm unlikable and you're a nitwit. You know which line I was talking about."

I had to admit it. "All right . . . yes, the line played great."

"So you did the experiment."

"Yeah, I did it. And it worked. So what does that prove?"

He said, "I thought it would prove that I'm your guardian angel."

"Now who's being the nitwit? It didn't prove that at all. It didn't prove anything."

"There," he said. "You just won the nitwit championship back."

"I won the nitwit championship back?"

"Yeah." He held up his glass for a scotch refill. "I was going to buy my own drink this time, but now I'm going to let you buy it for being so dumb."

Dan brought the drink and I motioned for him to take the money from my bills on the bar. This guy was so laughable, he was entertaining. Buying a few drinks for him was worth it.

He sipped his drink and said, "This stuff is pretty damned good. I'm glad you put me on to it."

"You keep belting it down like that and you're going to get the nitwit championship back permanently. So tell me why I'm so dumb."

He complied readily. "Because you think our experiment didn't prove anything."

"It certainly didn't prove you're an angel."

"Forget me. I don't have to prove I'm your guardian angel. I'll do my job whether you believe me or not. The experiment should have proved something about you."

"Okay," I asked, somewhat intrigued, "what did it prove about me?"

"It proved that you could write one great joke."

"Oh wonderful," I said without trying to hide my sarcasm this time.

He said, "Did I not ask you last week to write one great joke?"

I said, "How come you're talking like Joe Pesci all of a sudden? Yes, you asked me last week to write one great joke."

"Did you not go home and work all week on that one great joke?"

"You're going to keep talking like Joe Pesci, huh? Yes, I did go home and work on one great joke."

"Did you not come up with a great joke?"

"Yes, I admit it, it was a great joke. It worked beautifully tonight."

"It will work beautifully every night, dummy, because it's a great joke."

I said, "So what does that prove? What am I going to do with one joke? What? Am I going to call Letterman and say 'Hey Dave, put me on your show. I've got a great joke!'"

I was getting a bit loud with my protestations so Dan gave me a warning look. I ignored him.

"What am I going to do? Headline in Las Vegas, and they'll announce, 'Ladies and gentlemen, all the way from Philadelphia, the fabulous Chuck Barry,' then I'll come out and do one joke? After that one joke I'll walk off and they'll say, 'Ladies and gentlemen, Chuck Barry has left the building.'"

He said, "That could happen."

"Maybe where you live—up in Heaven—that could happen," I said, a decibel or two louder than I should have. "Where I live—in the real world—you don't make it with one great joke."

"You don't make it with a lot of lousy ones, either," he said matching my amplitude. "That's what you had in your act before. Now you've got at least one great one. You're at least one joke better than you were last week."

I motioned for Dan to bring me another scotch... quickly. Dan brought the drink but cautioned us. "You guys gotta try to hold it down a bit. Other comics are still performing in the show room."

I said, "Sorry," and took a sip of my J & B.

We sat in silence for awhile, each of us occasionally either sampling our drink or just fiddling with the glass.

I finally said, "I'm sorry, Bill, but I don't see the point of this whole thing. Even that bartender said my one joke was great but the rest of my routine sucked."

Bill took a sip of his J & B and said, "Okay, you decide. Who are you going to listen to—a bartender or your guardian angel?"

"Well, I just don't see what difference one joke makes."

He raised his glass and said, "Congratulations."

I took the hint and clinked our glasses together and said, "For what?"

He said, "You just got the nitwit championship belt back again."

I said, unenthusiastically, "How did I accomplish that?"

"You totally missed the point of what I got you to do last week, what you did, what you can do in the future."

"I missed all of that?"

"Totally."

I said, "Well, since I'm the world's champion nitwit and you're blessed with knowing all there is to know, why don't you just tell me what I missed?"

He said, "I got you to write a great joke."

"That means nothing."

Bill slammed his hand down hard on the bar and shouted, "Nitwit. It means everything!"

I shouted right back at him, "How?"

Bill hollered back at me, "I told you, you go from lousy to good to great! You're one step closer to good than you were a week ago."

Dan came over again. "Guys, you have to hold it down or I'm going to have to ask you to leave."

Bill picked up his glass and drained the remainder of his drink. He said, "I think leaving here is a very good idea."

I agreed. I downed the last of my scotch and started to gather my change from the bar. Then I said, "Bill, I bought the drinks, why don't you leave the tip?"

He patted his pockets and said, "I'm sorry, I don't have change for a tip."

I said, "I thought you guys got a per diem."

He said, "We do, but you know God. He only pays in big bills. It's a status thing with Him."

What a deadbeat this phony angel was.

I dropped three dollars on the bar and we both headed out. Then I went back and took back one of the dollar bills. Why should I over tip a guy who thought my routine sucked?

Before we reached the door, Bill stopped me. In an apologetic tone of voice he said, "Can I ask you two questions?"

I took this as a signal of a truce. "Go ahead."

"First, have you ever heard of a cheese steak?"

I said, "Of course, I've heard of a cheese steak."

He said, "Next question. Can you take me someplace where I can get one? I'd like to talk to you a bit more."

"About what?"

"About what you really learned from your experiment."

CHAPTER FOUR...

FOR THE SECOND WEEK IN A ROW, WITHOUT KNOWING EXACTLY why, instead of being home in bed, I was sitting at a table watching a delusional man, who thought he was a cherubim or seraphim or one of those angelic divisions, devour with relish—I should say with delight, although he had relish on it, too—a Philadelphia cheese steak.

"These things are pretty damned good," Bill said.

I said, "You never had a cheese steak before?"

He said, "Never. You know who would love one of these? St. Anthony."

"St. Anthony? The guy who finds stuff?"

"Un, huh. He's Italian, you know."

"Yeah, I know."

"You should order one."

The aroma was tempting, but I said, "No thanks, I'll just have my coffee. It's too late for me to eat a cheese steak."

"No," he said with a mouthful of minute steak, cheese, fried onions, and Italian bread, "it's never too late for food like this. This cheese steak thing is pretty damned good. Why don't you do what I do?"

"What's that?" I asked.

"Just consider it an early breakfast."

"I've had cheese steaks. I'll have more. But you got me to come here because you wanted to talk."

"And because I wanted a cheese steak."

"Yeah, I know, but you were going to tell me what I learned from spending all that time writing one joke."

He wiped his mouth with his napkin and took a sip from his shake. He said, pointing to the shake, "These are pretty damned good, too. What do you call these?"

"It's a milk shake."

"I know, but what kind?"

"A black and white milk shake."

He said, "Pretty damned good." He took another gulp, wiped his mouth again and settled down for some serious talk.

He began with, "You know, you said something last week that fascinated me."

"Really?" I said. "You said absolutely nothing that fascinated me."

"I'm an angel. I'm a holy person. I'm going to ignore that remark. Besides I have a cheese steak in my hands so I'm in a good mood."

I said, "Okay, what did I say that caught your attention?"

"You said that you thought my job was to keep you from getting run over or having a safe fall on your head or something like that. Right?"

"I guess so. I don't really remember."

"Well, you're right. That's my official duty as your guardian angel. You're 24 years old and you're still alive, right?"

"Right."

"Okay, so I'm doing a pretty good job, right? Roseanne Barr used to do a joke like that. She said if her husband came home from work and the kids were still alive she thought she did her job."

"Funny."

"Yeah, it is. You haven't been hit by a car, have you?"

"Not lately."

"No safes have crashed on your head?"

"Not that I know of."

"And there was something else. Oh yeah, you haven't fallen out of tree, have you?"

"No," I said, "I've been lucky in that regard."

"Okay, then I've done my job. But I'm the kind of guardian angel who likes to go the extra mile, you know what I mean?"

"Absolutely not."

"I want to do more for you than just keep you alive and healthy."

"Thank you."

"You will thank me...eventually. And next time you'll mean it rather than being a smartass."

"What exactly is it that you're going to do for me?"

"What do you want most in the world?"

"A new guardian angel."

"I'm being serious here."

"Seriously?"

"What do you want more than anything else you can think of?"

"You know what I want. I love comedy. I want to make people laugh."

"There!" He rapped his knuckles on the table. "You are one lucky guy; you know what you want."

"And I want to make money at it," I quickly added.

"Would you believe that many people don't know what they want in life? They either haven't thought about it or they kid themselves into thinking they want something that they don't really want but they think they want because somebody else wants it for them?"

"Huh?"

Bill said, "Yeah, I know. It was a long, complicated sentence, but it makes sense. To get what you want, you have to know what you want. Otherwise how are you going to know when you've got it? But it has to be something that you really want. Not something that tradition says you should want, or your parents demand, or you think is the most profitable. Understand?"

"Yeah, I see what you're driving at. But this is something I really want."

"Good. That's what I said. You're lucky. I'm lucky too, because I'm loving this cheese steak." He took another bite. Our conversation stalled while he munched on the mouthful. Before he was quite done chewing, he mumbled on. "Now, I was going to help you remember what you learned from our experiment."

"Right."

"Okay, let's go back to your previous achievements— learning to walk and drive."

"For crying out loud, Bill. Every healthy adult on the planet knows how to walk and drive. Why do you keep harping on that?"

"Because the smart ones learn from it."

"They learn from it?"

"The smart ones do," he repeated. "And I'm going to help you to be one of the smart ones. In our experiment you wrote one good line for your act, right?"

"Yeah."

"It played well, didn't it?"

I agreed. "Yeah, the line about my dad and the golf cart got a big response."

"Why?"

I said, "Because it was funny."

"That's right. It was funny. And where did you get that line?"

"I wrote it. You told me to write it, so I wrote it. Maybe I should start writing things on napkins for you."

"Okay, forget about being a wiseguy for a minute. Let me ask you, was it the first line you wrote?"

"No, I worked all week on that one line."

"Why?"

"Because of you. You told me you wanted it to be a great line."

"Wasn't the first line you wrote great?"

"No. If it was I would have stopped there."

"Then the second line you wrote was great."

"Are we not communicating here?" I asked. "I told you I worked all week on it."

"So you kept going until you got it?"

"Yes." I was getting annoyed at how thick headed he was being.

"Now let's go back to when you learned to walk."

"You're absolutely obsessed with me learning to walk, aren't you?"

Bill continued right on regardless of whether I was becoming fed up or not. "How many times did you fall on your cute little backside when you were learning to walk?"

"How do you know my backside was cute?"

"I'm your guardian angel for crying out loud. I've seen your cute little backside more times than I care to remember."

"Then you should remember how many times I fell on it."

"It was quite a few, wouldn't you say?"

"I'm sure it was quite a few. What's the point?"

He ignored my question. "But you succeeded."

"I'm walking, ain't I?"

"You failed quite a few times before you walked. You failed quite a few times before you got your one big joke. What does that tell you about achieving a goal?"

Reluctantly, I had to admit that he was beginning to get his point across. "That you have to keep going, I guess."

"Bingo. That deserves to be memorialized on a paper napkin." He grabbed one from the dispenser and jotted on it. When he was finished, he tossed the napkin to me.

It read:

Persevere! If it's something you want, keep going until you get it.

Bill said, "There it is in black and white. You must persevere. You may not reach your goal the first time, or the second time, or even the tenth time. But if it's something you really want—something you really want—you keep going until you get it."

"You make it sound easy."

Bill pointed a finger at me. "Don't ever make the mistake of thinking it's easy. Was it easy for you to write that joke?"

"Hell, no. I didn't think I'd ever get it on paper."

"But you did. Remember that—there's a difference between easy and achieving."

Bill took the last bite of his cheese steak and washed it down with the milk shake. He kept sipping the shake until he was sucking air.

"That was great. It's like finishing a good book. You're glad you finished it, but you're disappointed that you have nothing more to read."

"Or in your case, to eat. You want another one?"

"Of course, I want another one, but thankfully I'm blessed with angelic self-discipline, so I'll just have a cup of coffee instead." He signaled the waitress and ordered his coffee.

"Now," he said, "we'll move on to your success at driving."

"I wouldn't call it a success."

"You're driving, aren't you?"

"Of course I'm driving."

"Then you were successful. It's an achievement. When you learned to drive you were a little bit older than when you learned to walk, I assume?"

PERSEVERE !
IF IT'S SOMETHING
YOU WANT, KEEP
GOING UNTIL YOU
GET IT.

"Yeah, they have a law about that down here on earth."

"So you knew enough to give up if things weren't working out, right?"

"Things did work out, though. I did learn to drive."

"Did you zoom out onto the Schuylkill Express and zip in and out of traffic the first time you put your car in gear?"

"No."

"So you weren't a very good driver the first time you tried it."

I had no idea where he was going with this. "No, I suppose I was not a good driver for awhile."

"So why didn't you quit? Why didn't you just give up?"

"Why would I give up? I knew I could drive. I know a lot of stupid people in this world and they all have driver's licenses. I knew if they could do it, I could do it."

Bill rapped his knuckles on the table again. "Bingo," he said. He startled the waitress who was delivering his coffee. She spilled some of it as she was setting it down. She mopped up the mess with a napkin she pulled from a pocket in her apron and walked away from the table shaking her head at the loonies she had to wait on at this hour of the morning.

Bill sipped the hot, fresh coffee and said, "Does that give you another hint about what you need in order to achieve a goal?"

"You have to believe you can do it."

"You have to know you can do it." He started writing on another napkin. Then, he held his note up for me to see. It said:

You must believe—you must know—that you can achieve what you want.

Bill went on. "You knew you could learn to drive, didn't you?"

"Of course. As I said, all those other idiots did it."

YOU MUST BELIEVE
—YOU MUST KNOW—
THAT YOU CAN
ACHIEVE WHAT
YOU WANT.

"That's quite a compliment you just paid yourself—'If other idiots could learn to drive, so could I.'"

"That was a cheap shot, Bill."

"I know. I know. Only kidding. But let's review. To achieve something you need an honest desire. You must really want it. You must sincerely believe you can accomplish it—to the point of knowing you can accomplish it. Then you must persevere."

I put it in my words to see if I understood his message. "So, if I want something badly enough, convince myself I can get it, and keep on trying, then I'll get it."

"I didn't say that."

Now I was confused all over again. "Then what the hell are you saying?"

Bill said, "Let's use as an example someone who has achieved honest to goodness excellence. Someone who went from lousy to good to great."

I signaled the waitress for a refill of my coffee cup. This story was going to take even more time. A good night's sleep for me was becoming more and more remote.

Bill went on. "Let's take a youngster who has risen to the top of his profession, surpassed everyone along the way. He has fame, fortune, celebrity and pretty much anything else you can think of."

I asked, "Are we talking about Clark Kent or Superman?"

Bill said, "I'm talking about Tiger Woods, arguably the greatest golfer of all time. Why is he that?"

"I'm sure you're going to tell me."

"Many people respond to that question by saying, 'Because he's got God-given talent.'"

"You don't agree he has God-given talent?"

"I was talking to God about that the other day."

"Bill . . . that is the ultimate in name-dropping—'I was talking to God the other day.'"

"Well, I know Him. We talk about sports a lot. Anyway, God said, 'I didn't give him the talent.' So I says to God, 'Then where did he get it?' So God says to me, 'He bought it.'"

I was incredulous at this fabrication. "He bought it? God sells golf skills?"

"God sells everything. Whatever you want, it's for sale."

"What is He? Like a divine eBay?"

"That's funny. I'll have to tell Him that one."

"What do you mean—he bought it?"

"Anything you want is for sale. But—and I warn you it's a big 'but'—it has a price tag attached."

"A price tag?"

"That's right. Tiger Woods paid the price."

"What price are you talking about?"

"Tiger hit thousands of golf balls. He hit from the range, from the rough, from the sand. He put in hours perfecting his swing. He ate right, he exercised, he kept his body in perfect shape for golf. He did whatever his goal demanded of him. He paid the price. He bought his success."

Bill ripped another napkin from the dispenser.

I said, "I'm glad this place doesn't charge by the napkin."

Bill ignored me and kept writing. When he was done, I read the advice he had written for me:

You must be willing to pay the price

Bill said, "So now we're back to you. What you want to achieve has a price tag hanging from it, too. Are you ready for another experiment to see if you're willing to pay the price?"

"What kind of experiment?"

"You wrote one great joke for your act last week. How would you like to have five terrific gags for your act next week?

"Of course, I'd like that. What comic wouldn't, but what's the catch?"

"Last week you wrote one great joke. You did a good job of it. Now I want you to write more."

"How much more?"

"Write ten jokes a day."

"What?" This was getting insane. "I almost pulled a brain muscle writing one great joke. Now you want me to write ten great jokes every day?"

"I didn't say ten great jokes. Just write ten jokes every day for the next week. They can be good, bad, or indifferent, it doesn't matter. Just be sure to write ten a day. Are you willing to try that?"

"They don't have to be great?"

"No. They just have to be ten."

"Yeah, I can do that. But what if all the jokes are awful?"

"You'll discover the answer to that question as you write them. Now pay the bill, go home, and get some sleep."

He left.

I paid the bill.

YOU MUST BE
WILLING TO PAY
THE PRICE

CHAPTER FIVE...

I DID WHAT BILL ASKED ME TO DO. THERE HAD TO BE AT LEAST ten gags written on my yellow legal pad before I'd permit myself to retire for the night. A few times, I confess, I rushed through them. After all, Bill told me that the jokes didn't have to be good; they just had to be ten.

Sticking to a quota like that did teach me a few things about writing. It taught me that it's damned hard work to turn out ten gags a day. I felt like the top of my head was going to blow off. But I got them done.

I also learned what Bill meant when I wondered what would happen if all the jokes turned out terrible. He told me "You'll discover the answer to that question when you write them." And I did. Sure, Bill said that the material could be good, bad, or downright awful, but you can't just put a crummy joke on paper. At least, I couldn't put a crummy joke on paper. If you care about your comedy, you can't do that to yourself. I mean, it would be like your mother purposely trying to cook a bad family meal. So that was a tricky little move on my "guardian angel's" part.

That's something else I learned—the man had quite a few tricky moves. The whole thing had been a con man maneuver on his part. Figure the odds. You write ten gags a day for seven days, you've got seventy jokes. Of course, you get maybe five pretty damn good ones out of that kind of production.

And I did get some good lines. I played the Cherry Hill Comedy Cabaret the next weekend. I used the new material and it played great. Why? Because they were pretty damn good comedy lines.

Well, here. Judge for yourself. (Remember, though, you're hearing these without the benefit of my charming delivery and impeccable timing.)

In the routine about what a cheapskate my father was, I told the audience:

My Dad borrows money from everybody. The message on our family answering machine is "Hi. Your check's in the mail."

Dad is so cheap he won't even buy deodorant. He buys soap that odor-proofs the body for 12 hours . . . and keeps turning his watch back.

Dad hates to part with money. He has the only wallet I've ever seen that comes with a freezer compartment.

Once we went on a family vacation and Dad booked the cheapest airline he could find. When we got on the plane and they rolled those little steps away . . . the plane fell over on its side.

Dad finally bought a car, but now he's too cheap to buy gas. Instead he bought a map that shows you how to get anywhere in the United States by going downhill.

The audience loved it. They laughed in all the right places. And I loved the routine because the audience loved it. The sound of laughter is lovable.

The real test, though, was to see what Bill thought of the material. Would he love it? I ordered my usual scotch after my gig, not because I wanted one so much, but because I'd learned that's what brought my guardian angel out of hiding. You know, I never saw him in the audience, laughing, applauding, smirking, heckling, nothing. But afterwards, he'd appear and offer some criticism and collect his free drink or two. As soon as my drink arrived, so did Bill. Like a moth drawn to the flame, my guardian angel was attracted by the smell of scotch. I ordered one for him.

"How'd you like the new material?" I asked.

"I don't care about the new material."

"But it played great."

"I don't care if it played great."

"What the hell is going on here? You have me busting my ass to write material and then you don't give a damn about it."

He gave me a "naughty-naughty" sign by wagging his finger at me. "You shouldn't say 'ass' to an angel."

"Why not?"

"Because we don't have one."

I glanced around and looked behind him. "What's that you're sitting on?"

"It's not mine," he said.

"You're sitting on someone else's ass while you're drinking somebody else's scotch?"

"It's not somebody else's. It's the appearance of an ass. I'm pure spirit; my whole body is an apparition."

I said, "Bill, I've walked behind you out of several clubs and restaurants. Trust me. Your ass is not an apparition."

Bill took an extra long sip of his scotch and said, "Can we forget about my behind?"

"Please, let's do."

"Let's get back to what we were talking about. What were we talking about?"

I reminded him, "Why I'm working my tail off and you don't seem to care."

"Oh yeah," he said, then savored some more of his J & B. "Did your mother care that your first baby step looked like a cocker spaniel standing on its hind legs begging for a doggie bone?"

"Now we're back to me learning how to walk again." This guy was infuriating.

"Let me explain something—what you do and how you do it is less important than the fact that you do it. That's what really counts."

"Let me get this straight—you don't care if I go out there and bomb."

"You already have and you will again."

"Wow, you must be one helluva guardian angel. 'Hey, I don't give a damn whether you get hit by a truck or not. There's an 18-wheeler coming, but go ahead and cross the street. Be my guest.'"

"Whether you bomb on certain nights or not has nothing to do with your progress toward your goal."

I sometimes felt that Bill just enjoyed confusing me. I said, "You keep telling me that I should go from lousy to good to great. How can I do that if I keep bouncing back to lousy again?"

"Chuck, you're going to have good nights on stage and you're going to have bad nights. Any comic who tells you he's never had a bad show is lying. That's part of the game."

I couldn't believe his indifference. "Then how come you were so tough on me that first night when you kept telling me I was lousy?"

"I wasn't tough on you. I was just telling you that you were lousy. That was the truth; you were."

"So how come you get so vocal when I'm lousy, but you don't even notice when I'm good?"

"Let me ask you a hypothetical question. Suppose the jokes you added to the act tonight were terrible."

"They weren't."

"Suppose they were."

"They weren't."

"Buy me another scotch because the conversation is starting to stall here."

I motioned for another round . . . and, of course, paid for them.

We both drank.

Bill said, "Now let me say it again. This is a hypothetical question. Suppose the material tonight was lousy." He added quickly before I got a chance to jump in again, "I know it wasn't, but suppose it was. What would you do then?"

I answered honestly, "I don't know."

"Let me give you a hint," Bill said. "The first few baby steps you took were terrible. What did you do then?"

"How do you know my first few baby steps were terrible? Maybe I was a natural."

Bill laughed. "I was there. Trust me they were terrible. But what did you do then?"

"I tried again."

Bill lifted his J & B and said, "Let's toast to that comment." We clinked glasses.

Bill went on. "Remember this point and it'll serve you well—there's no shame in being lousy. The only shame is in staying at the same degree of lousiness or getting discouraged and giving up completely."

"Okay, I understand perseverance, but you keep talking about lousiness—if that's a word—but I was pretty hot tonight. So what do I do then?"

"Same thing. You keep going. You keep writing to a quota. You stick with it and you make the next batch even better."

"When does it end?"

"This conversation ends right now because I'm hungry. Take me to that diner again. I feel like another cheese steak and a black and white shake. Wait. No, I think I'll have a vanilla shake this time."

"You're picking up the check this time, too."

He patted his pockets to indicate that they were empty. "I can't this time, Chuck."

"Man, you're killing my finances, you know that?"

"Look, it'll be worth it for you because tonight I'm going to teach you the infallible, irrefutable, unassailable, one-size fits all secret of success."

"If you know so much about getting what you want, why can't you find a way to get enough money to at least pay your share?"

"Chuck, I promise you I'll pay my share, but I'm a little light this week."

"What happened to your per diem?"

"We angels have expenses. Do you have any idea how much it costs to retune a harp?"

I had never heard that excuse before. Of course, I had never hung around with angels before.

Bill said, "Leave a nice tip for the bartender and let's go."

CHAPTER SIX...

BILL HAD THE SAME SANDWICH HE HAD THE PREVIOUS WEEK— a cheese steak with everything. This night, though, for whatever reason that prompts angels—or people who think they're angels—to do things, he had a vanilla shake. He chomped into the sandwich and seemed to be enjoying it even more this time around. He said, "You know a question we angels get a lot is 'What is Heaven really like?' Well the next time somebody asks me that, I'm going to tell them to have a Philly cheese steak, and with the first mouthful, they'll know what Heaven is really like."

He seemed to be proud of that bon mot. He washed both his wisdom and his cheese steak down with a hefty slurp of milk shake.

"Aren't you going to have one?" Bill asked.

"No, thanks. At this time of night I'm happy with my coffee."

He said, "I told you before—just pretend it's an early breakfast."

I said, "You know what I will have, though."

"What's that?" He somehow managed to get the words out past the partially-chewed steak and provolone.

"I will have that secret you promised me—the unfailing, unarguable, whatever the hell else you said about it, secret of success."

"Ah, yes," Bill said. "I'm glad you asked." Bill set his sandwich down on his plate and wiped his hands on a paper napkin. Like Pontius Pilate he cleansed his hands before making this momentous pronouncement.

Bill said, "I want you to think back a bit."

"To when I first learned to walk?"

"No, not quite that far this time."

"Good." I was relieved.

"Think back to the first time you and I met. Remember? I said you were lousy."

"You say that a lot. There are two things you say a lot—'You were lousy' and 'This stuff is pretty damned good.'"

Bill picked up the sandwich and bit off another big chunk. He wiped his hands again after setting it down. Some more food-garbled words came out of his mouth. They sounded like, "When I said you were lousy, what did you say?"

"I don't remember."

"You told me it was a bad audience."

"I think it was that night."

"It doesn't matter. If you want to advance, if you want to achieve anything, you have to assume responsibility. Whatever happens, good or bad, is because of you. You can't blame the audience. You can't claim it was because you had a lousy childhood."

"I didn't."

He ignored my objection and started writing on a napkin again. He spoke as he wrote, "You can't blame your agent or your manager. You can't claim that people are being unfair. From now on, the burden is squarely and totally on one Chuck Barry."

He held up the note for me to see. It read:

Whatever happens—good or bad—is your responsibility

"I don't understand," I said. "Why do I have to be responsible for everything that happens?"

WHATEVER HAPPENS
— GOOD OR BAD —
IS YOUR
RESPONSIBILITY

"Remember how we talked about when you learned to walk and drive..."

"Oh, no! We're back to those again."

"...you kept going and didn't give up until you achieved what you wanted to achieve."

"Perseverance. Yeah, I remember."

"Well, if you can get away with blaming other people—your parents, your manager, your agent, your audience—then you give yourself an excuse to quit. It's always their fault. But if you accept the responsibility, then it's not so easy to give up."

"Now wait a minute," I protested. "Suppose I do get a crowd that just doesn't like me?"

"Then it's up to you to find a way to make them like you or to find a new audience. Complaining that they don't like you does nothing to help you achieve your goals."

"Suppose I get a club owner that just won't book me?"

"Is your career so fragile that it depends on one club? Work other clubs."

"But suppose . . ."

Bill cut me off cold. "Suppose nothing. Whatever happens—whether it's fair or unfair—you have the responsibility of dealing with it. Why do I waste ink and napkins writing these things out if you're not going to pay attention to them?"

I said, "They're not even your napkins."

He ignored me. "Read the napkin I just gave you."

I did. I read it in a sing-songy fashion, like a kid memorizing something in school. "Whatever happens—good or bad—is your responsibility."

I added, "Just because you write something on a napkin doesn't make it so."

He just stared at me with a mixture of disbelief and anger in his eyes. "Yes, it does," he said.

I still wasn't ready to surrender. "But suppose..."

He jumped in before I could finish. "Whatever problem you're about to suppose, you have to either turn it to your advantage or find a way of working around it. Whining is a total waste of your energy and serves absolutely no purpose at all."

"But . . ."

"Either fix it or deal with it. End of discussion."

"I'm sorry, Bill, but this isn't sitting right with me. It doesn't seem fair."

"Okay, let me pose a hypothetical. You know what that word means, don't you?"

"You're one obnoxious angel, you know that? Just give me the hypothetical."

"Okay, suppose you're waiting for the subway at the Susquehanna stop. It's crowded, people all over the place. Suddenly someone pushes you onto the tracks, and the train is coming at you at seventy miles an hour."

"You're my guardian angel, why'd you let that happen?"

"Cut the wisecracks and stay with me on this. The train is zooming down on you, you're going to be smashed like a pumpkin. People are shouting for you to get off the tracks. Got the picture?"

"Yeah," I said.

"Okay, then, what do you do? Do you say, 'I'm not going to do anything. It's not my fault I'm here. Somebody pushed me?' Or do you scramble to get the hell out of the way of that train?"

"I'd get off the tracks as quick as I could."

"Even though it was someone else's fault that you're there?"

"Sure."

"That's the same thing you do when something unfortunate happens, whether it's fair or unfair, your fault or someone else's—you make it something that you deal with. Got it?"

"Let me ask you a hypothetical, now—suppose you get a guardian angel who is a real pain in the ass."

"Fortunately, you don't have that problem. Do we agree that you're responsible for everything from here on out?"

"I don't seem to have much choice."

Bill pointed his milk shake at me and said, "That's one of the wisest things you've said since I've known you." He siphoned a quarter of the milk shake up through the straw in one draw.

I took a swallow of coffee to celebrate the unusual compliment aimed at me. Or was it sarcasm? I said, "You were supposed to give me the unfailing secret of success."

"Yeah," Bill mumbled, chewing again. "But I didn't want to give you such a valuable potion if you weren't prepared to be the guy who was willing to do the work and accept the responsibility."

I said, "Wait a minute. I have to do work? I thought this was some heavenly secret you had that was going to get me whatever I wanted just with the snap of my fingers."

"There's no such thing, Chucky Boy. There's all sort of potential out there, not just for you but for anybody, everybody. But whoever wants it has to do the work. I've already written this on a napkin for you. It said, 'You must be willing to pay the price.' That price always involves some work."

"Okay, Bill," I said, "I was only trying to do a joke...but I guess it didn't go over so well."

"A lot of your jokes don't."

"Now who's doing bad jokes?"

He owned up to it. "Okay, I'm sorry. But do you agree that you're willing to do the work and accept responsibility?"

I put my left hand on the sandwich on his plate, raised my right hand, and said solemnly, "I swear on your steak sandwich."

He smacked my hand away. "Don't take my cheese steak's name in vain."

"Okay," I said. "I understand that I have to do the work and that I will accept the responsibility for whatever happens, good or bad, in sickness and in health, for richer or for poorer . . ."

"Stop making fun of this. This secret could change your life. Do you believe that?"

I said, "I can't believe anything until you tell me what the hell the secret is. I think you're just stalling so I'll buy you another steak and shake."

"No, no," he said. "It was delicious, but I can't handle another one."

"Why not?" I said. "Just pretend it's an early lunch."

"You're very irreverent for a mere mortal, you know that?"

"Sorry."

"I am ready for a cup of coffee now, though." He waved down the waitress.

He remained quiet while the waitress filled our cups and we both drank. I looked at him as if to say, "I'm waiting."

"Okay," he said. "Here's the secret of success, not just in comedy, but in anything you or anyone else wants to achieve."

Now he gave me a smug look as if he expected me to jump up and down and applaud the momentous wisdom he had just imparted.

I said, "I'm still waiting."

"The secret is this—be good at what you do . . ."

"What?" I shouted. "Be good at what you do? That's like saying the secret of being successful is to be successful."

"You didn't let me finish, you nitwit. I was just pausing for effect, and you jump right in with your idiotic assumptions. It's a good thing you're a comic. With your timing, you'd make a terrible straight man."

"Okay, I'm sorry," I said. "Continue."

He did. "The secret of success is to be good at what you do . . . and to keep getting better."

We stared at each other. I said, "That's it?"

He said, "That's plenty. In fact, that's so important, I'm going to underline it for you."

He took out a felt-tip pen. "How come you always have a felt-tip pen handy?" I asked.

"I need them to keep track of my expenses."

"What expenses? You haven't paid for a single thing since I've known you."

He ignored me, covered up his pen, and tossed the new wisdom to me. Underlined, it read:

Be good at what you do and keep getting better

"That secret," he said, pointing to the napkin, "applies to anything. If you do something and you get better at it, what are you going to be?"

BE GOOD AT WHAT
YOU DO AND
KEEP GETTING
BETTER

"Better at what I do."

"Good answer. But then if you keep getting better, and then better still, and then even better than that, then what?"

"I'll be terrific at whatever it is."

"Excellent."

"Thank you," I said.

"I wasn't talking about your answer; I was saying that eventually you'd be excellent at what you do. That's why writing that one great joke was so important. Because it got you started towards getting better."

"Oh, I see."

"I hope you do, because excellence—in any endeavor—cannot be denied. And that's the secret of achieving whatever you want. Does it make sense?"

"Yeah. I only have two questions."

"Go ahead."

"How do I get good at what I want to do and how do I go about getting better at it?"

Bill said, "Excellent. And now I am talking about your response. Those are very good questions...and, as they say on television, I'll have the answers to them when we come back."

"What?"

"Thanks for the meal, and I'll see you next time." He got up to leave.

I fumbled in my pocket for money. "Wait a minute. What should I do in the meantime?"

"Keep writing those ten jokes a day. It'll help make you a better writer. And that's the secret—get better, and better, and better." He continued to mutter "...and better, and better, and better..." as he walked out.

I settled the bill.

CHAPTER SEVEN...

IMPRESSING BILL WAS MORE IMPORTANT TO ME NOW THAN IT was before. Claiming he didn't care how I did on stage, to me, was a big fib. He cared. He just concocted that tale of his to make a point. He cared and I cared whether he cared or not. It was interesting. Bill was a kook. He was a bona fide earthly flako, not a heavenly one. Yet I listened to what he said and I followed his prescriptions, even though it was considerable work.

He reminded me of this old guy I knew when I was a kid. This guy used to wander around the neighborhood teaching us kids how to catch and bat and throw a curve ball. We tolerated him but laughed at him when he left. Later we learned that he really was a major league baseball player when he was young. He knew what he was talking about.

Bill knew what he was talking about, too. What he said felt valid and, so far, it seemed to be working. My act was improving, and I don't mean just the jokes. Yeah, the jokes were better. I was writing more jokes, so I had better gags to pick from. But everything about my performing was improving. I had a better attitude, more confidence, more enthusiasm. I noticed it and my audiences noticed it. So did some other folks. Clubs were now offering me better gigs—even a fill-in emcee and a middle spot. There was an agent who said he was interested, hinting that he thought he might be able to land better opportunities for me.

That's why that week I continued to stick to the writing quota, like Bill advised, concentrating on developing still better lines.

My dad was the victim of most of my barbs the previous week, so now I gave my mother equal time. My mom was always obsessed with cleanliness. She harped on us kids about it all the time. So I did my quota of jokes about that and tried the stuff out at the Cabaret in Northeast Philly. The new gags went over great. They got big laughs. I did lines like . . .

My mother believed that cleanliness was next to Godliness. She used to keep my brother and me so clean we always thought we were for sale.

Mom always had us washing some part of our body or another. She never thought we were clean if we were dry.

Mom believed that "idle hands were the Devil's workshop," so she always put a bar of soap in them.

And Mom loved starch, too. She put starch in everything. I remember one day I sneezed and cut my nose on my handkerchief.

One night my brother fell out of bed and broke his pajamas.

Mom even starched my trousers. Anytime our class went into church, I had to get two of my friends to help me genuflect.

What did Bill think of the new lines? He never heard them. Or if he did, he didn't meet me at the bar afterwards to discuss them. I must confess I missed him. I never really believed that he was my guardian angel, but I kind of enjoyed playing with the idea that he might be.

Even though I didn't have his curmudgeonly guidance, I decided to continue with this experiment. It had worked so well these past few weeks, and I was kind of getting used to churning out the ten gags a day, that I thought I might as well. I concentrated the following week on another obsession of my mom's—having religious articles all over the house.

For my gig in Doylestown, I came up with material like...

We had statues of saints all over the place. Our living room looked like a Catholic Smithsonian Institute.

See Mom had a serious problem. She was a statue-a-holic.

I did this one especially for Bill . . .

We always had two statues of St. Anthony. That's right. You guessed it. The second one was so that we could pray to it whenever the first one got lost.

We had a large family. Mom and Dad slept in the St. Theresa room. The girls slept in the St. Maria Goretti room. And the boys had the St. Isaac Jogues room. Of course, every so often during the night, we'd all have to get up and visit the St. John.

The entire house was decorated in "early sanctity." Our house was burglarized four times, but nothing was ever stolen. We wound up with four converts.

Guardian angels you would figure would have to relate to material about religion, right? I thought Bill would rave about this stuff, but again he didn't show up for our cocktail-time conference after the show. Maybe Doylestown was a little too far for him to travel, but still something didn't feel right. I, for one, didn't feel right. There was kind of an empty feeling inside me that I couldn't quite explain or describe, but it was there. The material I'd written was good, it worked in the act, got nice laughs, still something was missing.

Oh, don't get me wrong I was glad the stuff was working and the audiences were laughing, but I wanted to impress Bill. I wanted him to see how well I had done, how the audiences were accepting the stuff. I wanted to show him that things had changed since the first night we sat and talked. I wanted him to sit next to me one time and honestly say, "You were pretty damn good." Yeah, that's right. I wanted to get the same compliment from him that he gave to cheese steaks. But he didn't show.

He didn't show up on the following weekend, either. I was beginning to worry that maybe I did something to offend him—to drive him away. But then I thought, aw, maybe they just had a guardian angel convention in Toronto, or something like that. Still, to be perfectly honest with you, I was worried that something might have happened to him.

He seemed to have just disappeared and I didn't know where or how to find him. In fact, I didn't even know his last name. He was just "Bill" or "Archangel Shecky."

Do you believe this? I may be the only Catholic in the world who worried that something bad might have happened to his guardian angel.

CHAPTER EIGHT...

FINALLY MY GUARDIAN ANGEL REAPPEARED. I DON'T MEAN "reappeared" in the sacred or holy sense like Our Lady of Lourdes or Our Lady of Fátima. I just mean he finally showed up. He wasn't there for my Friday or Saturday night sets, but after my last performance on Sunday night, I was sipping a coke at the bar (subliminally I must have felt guilty about drinking scotch without Bill drinking along with me) when someone behind me said, "You've got some nice new material in there."

I recognized the voice, so before I finished turning to face him I said, "Where the hell have you been?"

He ignored me long enough to motion to the bartender, "I'll have what he's having." Then he saw what I was having. He quickly added, "No, I won't. I'll have a J & B on the rocks." A few weeks ago he claimed he had never even tasted scotch; now he had a favorite brand.

"Well?" I wanted an answer to my question. I deserved an answer to my question.

"What?" He pretended innocence.

I repeated, "Where the hell have you been? I've been worried sick about you."

"Hey," he said, "I'm the guardian angel, remember? You're just my assigned nitwit."

I still wanted an answer. "Where were you?"

The bartender served his scotch. Bill sipped it with his usual comment, "This stuff is really pretty damned good."

I said, "I asked where you were."

"I was doing guardian angel stuff."

"Like what?"

He sipped again and said, "Like catching up on my paper work."

What a fraud this guy was. I said, "I thought you angels communicated with thoughts, mental telepathy, and stuff like that."

He said, "Yeah, we do. But we like to keep a hard copy, just for reference and backup, you know."

"Oh? And where do you keep all this stuff?"

He shook his head and said, "You people really are nit-wits. Heaven's a big place. You don't think we have room up there for a filing cabinet?"

The argument was getting pointless so I abandoned it, but I still wanted him to know I was a little put off by his disappearance. "I wish you would have told me you were going to go away for awhile. Would that have been too much trouble?"

He said, "Hey, I'm sorry." He seemed genuinely contrite, too. "Let me buy you a drink."

I said, "I'll buy my own drink, thank you." I signaled to the bartender and added, "The same as he's having."

"I can't buy you a drink? What? Are you going to hold a grudge now?"

"No, I'm not holding a grudge. It's just that you've got a perfect record so far of not paying for anything and I don't want to end the string."

The bartender set my drink down and lifted some of my cash off the bar. Bill didn't object. He said, "Now that you've got a real drink, I can do this."

He picked up his glass and held it up to me. He said, "Truce?"

I clinked my glass against his and said, "Truce."

We both sipped to our cease-fire.

Bill broke the moment of silence that followed. "You got some new material in your set."

I said, "How do you know that? I never see you in the audience. I never hear you laughing or applauding. I only see you when you're hungry or thirsty. How do you know I have new stuff and how do you know it's any good?"

He explained it away simply. He said, "I'm an angel. I see all things; I know all things."

My early catechism training in the Catholic school system prompted me to say, "I thought only God knows all things."

Bill said, "Nah, we just let Him think that."

"You let Him think that? Isn't that the attitude that got Lucifer sent to the Minor Leagues?"

Bill said, "Yeah, but I'm only kidding. Lucifer was serious."

"I don't know if you know all things or not," I said, "but you are right about one thing—I have been writing some nice stuff lately."

"That's right, you have," Bill said. "Do you know why?"

"Why?"

"Because I taught you how, that's why."

I said, "I should come up with a great put-down line right now but I can't. I have to be honest with you. The things you've told me have made a big difference. I know it and the audience seems to know it."

Bill said, "When I first met you, you wanted to get out of the comedy business."

"Well, now things are going a lot better."

"So, you still want to be a comedian?" he asked.

"Yeah."

"Are you sure?"

"Yeah, I'm sure."

He asked, "Are you sure you're sure?"

With a touch of irritation I said, "I'm sure I'm sure and if you ask me if I'm sure about that then I'll say 'Yes, I'm sure I'm sure I'm sure.'"

"I'm just double checking because you know there's nothing wrong with changing your mind. Once you set a goal for yourself, it's not carved in stone. You can always change it to a different goal."

"I definitely want to be a comedian, Bill."

Bill, the guardian angel/curmudgeon said, "Okay, I just wanted to double check. We still have a lot more work to do, though."

"We? What are we—a team now? Are we going to start arguing over who gets top billing? Who gets 60 percent and who gets 40 percent?"

Bill deliberately took a long sip of scotch to add a bit of drama to what he was about to say. The man had a flair for showmanship. "Let me ask you something," he said. "Who wrote the new material you've got in your act?"

"I did," I said. "Every bit of it."

He went on. "When I ask you to try something new, who does it?"

"I do."

He said, "Damn right you do, and don't you ever forget that. Whatever you expect to get in this life or in your career, you're going to have to get it. We talked about this before, but you've forgotten it already. You're going to have to be the one who does the work. And you're going to be the one who gets 100 percent of the rewards. Do you understand that?"

Wow, I had never heard him quite this intense before. It confounded me a bit. I answered, "Yeah, I guess I do."

"Will you remember it?"

"I'll remember it."

He said, "Okay, then. Buy me another scotch because I want to talk to you about something."

I signaled for two more. I said, "All right now, what's so important that I had to pay for another round?" They came quickly and more of my money went quickly.

"I had to go away for a reason."

I said, "I knew it. What's wrong?"

He said, "Don't worry about that. Handling what's wrong is my job. But you and I have to start working a little harder and a little faster."

"Why?"

"Because...well...because we don't have much more time."

Boy, that got my attention. "What do you mean—we don't have much more time?

Bill said, "I can't go into that right now. You'll just have to trust me."

"Wait a minute. If you say that we don't have much more time, that means that something is going to happen to one of us. Since you claim to be an angel and have life everlasting, I can only assume that I'm going to get hit by a truck."

"Boy, you people really are nitwits. They say that you humans use only about ten percent of the brain that the Good Lord gave them. I think right now you're down to about point-six percent. Would I be working this hard to teach you a few tricks if you were going to get splattered all over the Schuylkill Expressway?"

"Well, then why don't we have time?"

"It's secret angel business. I could tell you, but then I'd have to kill you."

"You, an angel, would have to kill me?"

"That's right, and trust me, it wouldn't be pleasant. We do most of our killing with the jawbone of an ass."

"Then let's not do it," I said.

Bill turned his bar stool so he was facing me directly instead of his beloved scotch. He leaned towards me and tapped me on the knee. The talk suddenly was becoming more intimate. "Here's my plan. I want to have a tutoring session with you at least once a week."

"Oh, I get it now. This is Archangel Shecky's School of Comedy."

"Chuck, I'm teaching much more than comedy. I'm teaching you lessons in achievement—lessons that will help you achieve any goal you set in life."

"I know, Bill. So what will you call these once a week lessons?"

Billl thought for a brief second or two and said, "How about Archangel Shecky's School of Comedy and Get What You Want-iveness."

"That's a very clever title. How much is it going to cost me?"

"No charge."

"Then why are you doing it?"

"We guardian angels can't help ourselves."

"You're so full of crap."

"You said yourself that what I've told you has made a big difference."

I admitted it had.

He said, "What I'm going to teach you will make a bigger difference. Are you willing to give it a try?"

"No charge, right?"

"No charge. Are you in?"

"Why not? When do we start?"

"Tomorrow morning."

What he taught me had made a difference in my act, but not much in my salary. I still had to drive a truck to make a living. "I have to work tomorrow morning."

"We'll meet for breakfast. We'll talk, I'll teach. We'll finish up in plenty of time for you to make it to work."

It sounded workable. I said, "Okay, where?"

He said, "Let me ask you something. What is scrapple?"

"Don't tell me you've never tasted scrapple."

"Never have. What is it?"

"I could tell you, but then I'd have to kill you."

He chuckled. "But you eat it for breakfast, right?"

"Yeah, with ketchup and scrambled eggs and such."

"I want to try it," he said. "You tell me a place that serves great scrapple and I'll meet you there at 6:30 tomorrow morning."

I said, "Oh, so it's not going to cost me anything and all of a sudden I'm buying breakfast for two."

"Don't worry about breakfast," he said. "Tomorrow's on me."

"Wow," I said.

"What?"

"This is your first miracle."

CHAPTER NINE...

WHEN I AGREED TO MEET WITH BILL, I DIDN'T REALIZE THAT 6:30 came so early in the morning. But there I was sharing breakfast with a faux-angel who had never heard of scotch, never tasted sticky buns, never eaten scrapple, and yet who was going to teach me to be the next comic wunderkind of the world.

I got there a minute or two before Bill. When he'd joined me in the booth, I took the liberty of ordering three scrambled eggs with a generous side of scrapple, a toasted bagel, and a cup of coffee for him. Me, I settled for a cup of coffee. I'm not that coordinated. I have trouble chewing and waking up at the same time.

The coffee, when it arrived, smelled wonderful and tasted even better. It hit the spot. I became a bit more coherent. I woke up enough to coach Bill on the fine art of covering scrapple with ketchup. He poured even more than I advised onto his scrapple and eggs, and sampled the meal. "This stuff is heavenly."

"And when you say heavenly, you know what you're talking about, right?"

"You got it."

He chewed and swallowed another mouthful ecstatically. He was the only person I knew who could chew estatically. He asked, "How long has this scrapple stuff been around?"

I didn't know. "I guess as long as pigs have."

"This stuff is pretty damned good. I've got to tell God about this."

"I thought God knows all things."

Bill mumbled over another mouthful of eggs and scrapple and ketchup, "He does, but I'm not sure He's tasted all things. He's got to taste this stuff."

I sipped my coffee. At this hour of the morning, to me, it was as heavenly as my guardian angel's meal.

Bill said, "Is that all you're going to have? It's on me remember."

I said, "How could I forget something like that, but no. This is fine for me. I'm not a big breakfast eater."

"Man, you don't know what you're missing," Bill said as he scarfed.

I had to get to work, though. "So when do we start the Archangel Shecky's School of Comedy."

He said, "The lessons have already started."

"What do you mean?"

"The first time we met I had you write one good joke, remember?"

"Yeah. And I wrote a pretty good one."

"That was the first lesson. It taught you focus. That's an important word for a comedy writer. Do you know why?"

I said, "I don't have to; you'll tell me."

"Remember when you were a kid, you would sometimes take a magnifying glass and hold it over a piece of paper and focus the sun's rays on one small spot?"

"Sure."

"What happened?"

"Eventually, the spot started to turn brown and then it would catch fire."

He said, "That's right!" with such enthusiasm that he spit a bit of his heavenly breakfast at me. I wiped it off with my napkin. His breakfast didn't seem so heavenly on my face. "When you concentrate energy on a small area, it increases in intensity."

I sipped some more coffee with a look on my face that said, yeah, that makes sense.

Bill went on. "Same thing with a garden hose. If you put your thumb over the opening, to make it smaller, the water comes out with more force, right?"

I said, "Right."

Bill said, "That's what happens when you focus your energy on one small comedic thought—you produce some great comedy."

I said, "I did come up with a pretty good gag."

"Damn right you did. And do you know why?"

"I thought you just told me why."

He said, "That was only part of it. That lesson also taught you another important thing that a comedy writer has to learn—don't quit too soon."

"What do you mean?"

"Writers always want to quit writing. Most of them would rather have written than write. So as soon as they come up with a comic idea or a half-baked one-liner, they quit and move on to the next one. By making you come up with a great line, you couldn't quit until you got something extra special."

"You're right. I did write a bunch of lines that I wasn't exactly happy with."

"That's what you have to do. Have you ever heard of Charles Schultz, the cartoonist?"

"Sure, the guy that created Peanuts."

"Right. He was talking about some other cartoonists once and he said, 'Why don't they work harder? Why do they put down their first thought? Why don't they think about it a little longer and break the surface a little better and try to improve it? Why do they settle for the first, easy ideas?'"

I said, "In other words, why do they quit too soon?"

"There you go."

I signaled the waitress for a coffee refill. Bill pushed his cup forward too and said, "Do you have any more of this scrapple?"

She said, "I can bring you a side order."

He said, "Yeah, that'd be good."

"Do they have a Weight Watchers up in Heaven?" I asked.

"We don't need it up there. The flowing robes and the wings make you look thinner. Now . . . let's get back to Archangel Shecky's School of Comedy."

"Okay," I said, thinking how strange it was that I was looking forward to more advice from a man with angelic pretensions.

"The next time I taught you what is probably the most important lesson any comedy writer—heck, any writer—can learn. I taught you to set a quota and stick to it."

I said, "Yeah, that's when you had me writing ten jokes a day—good, bad, or indifferent."

He said, "Doing that, faithfully, does several things. First, it gets you writing. The only way to get ten new jokes a day is to write them, right?"

"Right."

"And that teaches you to write. Some of the great writers from the past say that there are only three ways to learn to write—write, write, and write."

"I've heard that."

He said, "That's good, because it's accurate. Each time you write, you learn a little more about writing. The more you write, the better you get at it, the easier it becomes. Writing something every day is a great home-study course in writing."

He stopped long enough to splatter ketchup on his freshly-delivered second helping of scrapple. The next thing he said was through a mouthful of semi-chewed pig parts. "And, writing every day keeps the comedy muscle limber."

"That you'll have to explain further."

"I know for a fact," he said, "that some of the writers on great TV variety shows would stop working real hard toward the end of the season."

I said, "They did?"

"Of course. During the season they would have to write several shows ahead. They always had to turn out new material. When the season was winding down, there were no shows coming up that they had to write for. Everything was already written."

"That makes sense."

"Everything I say makes sense," he said. "The writers on these staffs would then play games and amuse themselves. But...when something came up and they needed a joke, guess what?"

"What?"

"They couldn't write it. They had stopped being creative and it was hard to get it started again."

I asked, "Is that story true?"

He pointed a finger at me for emphasis. "Everything I tell you is either true or would be true if it had actually happened."

While I tried to figure the logic of that statement, he continued. "By sticking to a quota and writing every day, you actually make the writing process easier. Understood?"

"If you say so."

"Now you're learning. Since you're learning so well, you tell me another benefit of writing so many jokes regularly."

I turned my coffee cup as I tried to think of a correct response.

Bill said, "You, more than anybody, should know the answer to that."

"Why?"

He said, "You've already benefited from it."

"How?"

"Don't you have some new gags in your act?"

"Yeah, I do."

"How did they get there?"

"I wrote them."

"Bingo! When you write a lot of jokes, what do you wind up with?"

"A lot of jokes."

"You're a genius," he said. "Obviously, the more you write, the more material you're going to build up, the more you'll have to choose from. You'll lift the quantity of your writing and you'll improve the quality simply by improving your percentages. Does that make sense?"

"Yeah, it does."

"It was a rhetorical question. I've already told you everything I say makes sense."

"You know something? You're the most arrogant angel I've ever met."

"Thank you. Now about the 'Get What You Want-iveness' part of our curriculum. You had some questions about that the last time we talked."

The waitress freshened both of our cups of coffee and took away Bill's scraped-clean plates. I was glad. Now we could converse without him spraying his breakfast at me.

After a swallow of coffee, I said, "You said that the secret of success was to be good and keep getting better. How do I start being good?" I quickly added before he began pontificating, "And can we do this without mentioning my learning to walk or drive?"

"Of course, but you answered your own question."

"How?"

"You start. In order to be good at anything, you have to start it."

"Well, duh."

"That's not as dumb a statement as you apparently think it is. Many people want something, but they never take any steps to get it. To achieve anything, you must start somewhere, anywhere. You don't want to talk about your first baby steps anymore so let's suppose you want to be an artist."

"I can't draw a straight line."

"So? Draw a crooked line and keep making it straighter."

"Clever."

"And true, but we'll get to that part of it later. You want to be an artist, so you start. You go to the store, you buy some paints, a few brushes, grab a couple of canvases, and you come home and paint."

"Those paintings will be terrible."

"Chances are they will. Your act was lousy, too. Remember?

"How can I forget with you around?"

"But you are painting. If you keep painting, you'll get good at painting. Remember the writers said the way to learn to write is to write, write, write? Well, the way to learn to paint is to paint, paint, and paint."

"But what if you just keep being lousy?"

"Then if you really want to paint, you'll begin to recognize that you're work is terrible. That's when you begin the next phase of the process—you get better."

"That's the big question I have for you—how do you keep getting better?"

We both finished up our coffee and called for refills. I thought to myself, I may never sleep again.

After we each had another mouthful of coffee, Bill continued. "Why do you think that I have you writing ten jokes a day? So you'll keep getting better and better and better at it. How do you succeed?"

"Be good at what you do and keep getting better."

"Perfect."

"Okay, I know I'm getting better at comedy because the audience is laughing more. But let's get back to the painting. How would I know if I'm getting better at that?"

Bill said, "Good question and the crux of this 'Get What You Want-iveness.' You begin with an honest evaluation of yourself and your talent. You ask yourself if you're a good painter or not."

"And suppose the answer is no?"

"In the beginning, it probably will be. But now ask yourself why."

"That's easy. Because I don't know what I'm doing."

"That's probably right, too. So you get some training. Then you'll begin to learn what you have to know. And even as you start to learn what you have to know, you'll learn something else, too."

"What's that?" I asked.

Bill said, "You'll learn that no matter how much you know, you'll always know that there's even more that you don't know."

"Boy, you do like convoluted sentences, don't you."

"They get your attention and get my point across. And it's a very important point for anyone who wants to achieve anything."

"And that point is?"

"I'm going to write it down for you because it's another one that I want you to remember."

He put magic marker to paper napkin. When he was done, he showed me the note:

Always continue to learn

"Wonderful. I'm practically a pauper but I'm going to have to hire some great artist to give me lesson after lesson after lesson. What if I can't afford it?"

"Our last lesson, and your promise, was about you taking responsibility for your career. Now you're blaming the lack of money. That's not taking responsibility. That's against the rules."

"If I don't have money, I don't have money."

"Turn it to your advantage or work around it. Money, or lack of money, is a very popular excuse, but it's rarely valid."

"Then how do I get the training I need?"

"There are plenty of ways to learn without a professional instructor, although, if you can afford it, that's probably the best way."

"What are the other ways?"

"You can teach yourself. You can buy a book, and learn from that. You can get some instructional videos and use them for your education. You can observe others and imitate them. You can learn from trial and error. If you really want to improve, you'll find ways."

"I guess you're right there."

"No need to guess, Chuck. I'm always right."

"So all I have to do is get some education and I'll improve."

"No."

"Then what's the point you're making?"

"Once you learn the proper techniques, you have to apply them. You have to practice. You have to write, write, write, or paint, paint, paint, or do whatever it is you want to do over and over again. That's how you get better, better, better."

He was jotting on another napkin as he spoke. The napkin read:

Practice, practice, practice

"It sounds like hard work."

"I never said that getting what you want would be easy. But now you have to go back to an honest evaluation of yourself. Where do you still need improvement? Work on that. Once you improve in that area, what other areas do you have to work on?"

"When does it end?"

"It doesn't. Someone once said that success is a journey; not a destination. That pretty much sums it up. Let's look at Tiger Woods again. He's one of the most successful people of this era, yet he's constantly working on his game. He hires different coaches and practices relentlessly. As good as he is, he wants to keep getting better."

The waitress came over to refill our coffee cups. Both of us refused. I think both of us were getting a bit light-headed from the caffeine buzz. I know I was.

Bill said, "Now let's forget about painting and get back to what you do—comedy."

"Good."

"You've taken the first few steps. You already know this is something you want."

"Definitely."

"And that's good. You've started."

"Sure have. I've been doing comedy for several years."

"You recognized you were lousy."

"Not until you pointed it out to me—again, and again, and again."

"And you've got one of the greatest instructors you could possibly have."

"You?"

"Exactly. You're writing more and you're writing better. Now I'm going to teach you to write even smarter jokes."

"But the jokes I'm writing now are pretty good."

"Pretty good don't feed the bulldog."

"Someday we're going to have to have a lesson where you teach me what that phrase means."

"I'll do it right now. Pretty good is pretty good, but pretty good is never good enough."

"Bill, you're the only guy I know who can explain something by making it sound more complicated."

"Let me try to make it simpler. If you want to achieve something you've got to excel at it. You can't be as good as those who are already doing it. You have to be a tad better."

"Better?"

"That's right. You started by writing one great joke, then you started writing regularly and you turned out, as you say, pretty good material. Now you face the challenge of turning out superior material."

Bill started writing on a napkin again even before I asked the inevitable question—"How do I do that?"

He held up the napkin he had just written on. It gave me the answer.

Hone your technique

"What exactly does that mean?" I asked.

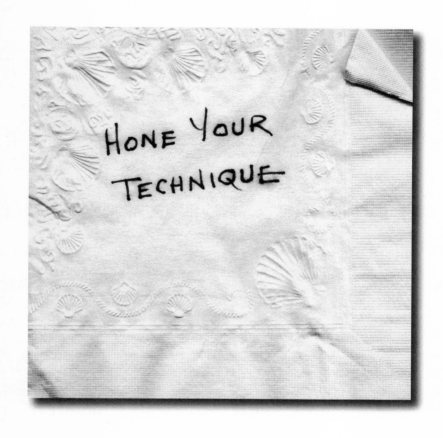

"I'm going to help you hone your writing technique now."

"This is today's lesson, I take it?"

"Yes it is, but remember that it applies to anyone who wants to achieve anything. You learn how to do it. You practice doing it. But then you go that extra step. You learn to develop your individual skills, to hone your particular technique. Do that in any profession and you'll be surprised at the results."

"So you're going to give me an example of how I can do this to achieve my particular goal?"

"That's right. This is one way of honing your writing skills. You may want to take notes."

I said, "I'll remember what you tell me."

"I hope you do. Today's lesson is this—tell the joke by not telling it."

"You wanted me to write that down?"

He said, "If you're smart, you'll engrave it right over the part of your brain that you use to write material."

"What does it mean?"

"It means that you let the audience write the end of the joke for you. They like doing that. It makes them part of the comedy. And when they do it, they surprise themselves and surprise is among the biggest components of comedy."

I said, "You're going to have to give me some examples of that."

He said, "Archangel Shecky would do nothing less. Here goes. Henny Youngman, you remember him?"

"Yeah."

"He had a joke that went, 'I haven't spoken to my wife in four years. I didn't want to interrupt.' Good line, right?"

I agreed.

Bill said, "Notice he doesn't say anything at all about how much his wife talks."

I disagreed. "Well, he does. He says he didn't want to interrupt."

"Exactly!" Bill shouted. "He implies that his wife talks a lot, but he doesn't say it. He let's the audience figure that out. He says it by not saying it. Brilliant."

"Yeah, I see."

"He could have said, 'My wife talks so constantly that I haven't been able to say anything for four years.'"

I said, "That's not funny."

"Right. Bob Hope used to do a line about all his travels. He said, 'Travel is very educational. I can now say Kaopectate in seven different languages.'"

"That's a funny line."

"Yes, it is." Bill was getting carried away with enthusiasm. "You notice he never says that he got sick during these travels."

"No, but he gets that idea across."

"He sure does. And that's what you want to do—say what you want to say by not saying it. Imply it and let the audience figure it out. Are you getting any of this?"

"Absolutely, I am," I said.

Bill finished the last of his coffee. I did, too. He said, "Okay, then, that's your homework assignment. Go through your act. Find statements and convert them to jokes. Find your punch line and imply it. Give the audience the thrill and the fun of figuring it out for themselves. We'll meet here again next Monday."

I was enthused about this lesson. I was eager to get working on it, but I also had to get to work and drive some candy around the city. However, I did remind Bill that this was his treat.

He said, "Absolutely." He picked up the check and called the waitress over. "Do you accept credit cards here?"

She said, "Yes we do."

"Master Card?"

"Yes, sir."

"All right, then. Bring me an application form."

I paid the tab.

Angels are devilish people.

CHAPTER TEN...

THAT NEW WRITING TECHNIQUE THAT BILL GAVE ME WAS fabulous. I made that a part of my joke writing the entire week, and I was so enthused I got to our breakfast meeting before Bill. That's quite an accomplishment when you beat him to food or drink.

I had my notes on the table right next to my cup of coffee when Bill came in. Before he even got fully seated, I sprung some of my newest gags on him. "Listen to this. I once had a blind date with a girl who was really skinny. She wore a strapless gown. I don't know what held it up...or why. See. I didn't really say she had small boobs, but I implied it."

Bill said, "Yeah, the joke's maybe a bit weak, yet that's the idea, but do you really think you should be talking about girls' boobs with an angel?"

"C'mon, you're not going to become a prude on me, are you?"

"No, but I'm going to make a point now that we're on that subject."

I knew what was coming. "Uh-oh, the fuddy-duddy speaks."

"This has nothing to do with being a fuddy-duddy and it has nothing to do with being a prude. It has everything to do with comedy. Stay away from the raunchy material and language."

"Bill, Lenny Bruce suffered to win the right to use expressive language on stage. Richard Pryor was a comedy genius and he . . ."

"I'm not talking about Lenny Bruce or Richard Pryor. I'm talking about you. I'm talking about anyone who is still learning. If you go for the easy, raunchy jokes now, you'll never grow as a humorist. You'll never do the work it takes to be truly funny. Once you learn to be funny, you can use any language you want."

I said, "But . . ."

Bill interrupted, "Enough said on the subject. I'm hungry and you have to get to work."

I should have known my omni-voracious guardian angel would prefer food to an intellectual argument. It would be futile to fight him on this.

I said, "Okay, you want to order something before I thrill you with the rest of my gags?"

He said, "Good idea."

"You going to have eggs and scrapple again?"

"I heard they have something here called Tastykakes."

"Philly's famous for them," I said.

The waitress came over to take his order. She brought a carafe of coffee with her and set it on the table.

He said, "I'll have those Tastykakes."

She said, "What kind?"

He looked at me. "They come in different kinds?"

"Yeah," I said, "they have butterscotch Krimpets, coconut. They even have Tastypies—apple, lemon, blueberry."

He said, "Krimpets?"

I said, "Yeah, they're little cakes. You get two of them in a package."

He said to the waitress, "I'll have them...the Krimpets."

She turned to leave, but he went on. "And that coconut cake...and an apple pie, a lemon, and a blueberry pie, too." She left shaking her head and he explained to me, "I haven't had breakfast yet."

It was only 6:45 in the morning. Nobody had breakfast yet.

But I had more jokes I was enthused about.

"Listen to this one," I said, "When I was in high school me and my friends would chase after anything wearing a skirt. Which explains why our high school band had to get rid of their bagpipe uniforms. See? I don't tell them we chased after the guys in kilts, but they get the picture."

He said, "Good. That's a funny image."

I went on. "Here's one I came up with about my girlfriend's lousy cooking. 'Let me tell you about my girlfriend's cooking. Her favorite dessert recipe begins: Take the juice from one bottle of Pepto-Bismol....' Then I follow it up with: 'In her kitchen the flies swat themselves.' I don't come out and say she's a terrible cook, but the audience gets the idea."

The waitress brought Bill's unusual order. She set down a plate with a package of Krimpets and a coconut Tastykake on one plate—all still unwrapped. On another plate were the apple, lemon, and blueberry Tastypies.

She said with a slight touch of sarcasm, "Can I get you anything else?"

Bill said, "Maybe later."

She walked away shaking her head. I suppose this diner wasn't used to serving ravenous angels.

Bill unwrapped the Krimpets first and bit into one.

Bill was interested in food; I was interested in my jokes. "Here's another one: 'I told my psychiatrist I thought every body hated me because I was so good looking. He said, You don't need a psychiatrist. You need a mirror.'"

"What do you think?"

"Pretty damned delicious."

"Tastykakes have been delicious for hundreds of years," I said. "I mean what do you think of these gags."

Bill seemed more intent on letting the taste of the butterscotch icing settle in. Finally he said, "What do you care what I think about your jokes?"

I was confused by that question. I said, "You're my mentor, my instructor in Archangel Shecky's School of Comedy."

"And of 'Get What You Want-iveness.' Don't forget that."

"Yeah, I just want to know if you like my jokes."

"Do you like them?"

I said honestly and enthusiastically, "I love them."

He said, "Then that's two percent of the job right there." He shoved the remainder of one of the krimpets into his mouth.

I said, "Two percent? Where's the other ninety-eight percent come from?"

He held his index finger up to me, gesturing that I'd have to wait until he finished chewing, swallowing, and savoring. Then he answered my question. "Schmuck. The audience. If they laugh, it's a great joke. If they don't laugh, it's a joke that either needs work or needs to be tossed away."

I scoffed at that. "Everybody knows that."

"No. Everybody does not know that. Some people write the jokes they want to write. Some comedians tell jokes that they think other comedians will like. So everyone doesn't know that the audience is the real judge of comedy. But now you do and that puts you a leg up on the competition. In other industries, it's the consumer who is the final judge."

With that lecture completed he began to open the coconut Tastykake and said, "Now we're ready to move on."

I said, "To the coconut one?"

"Yeah, that, too. But I meant to your next lesson." Then he took an angel-sized bite out of the cake. I sipped on my coffee realizing there wasn't going to be much conversation until he swallowed.

"This is even better than those Krimpets."

I said, "I do have to get to work today so maybe we can get to the next lesson."

He said, "You know what I like about these things?" He was referring to the cakes and pies before him.

I dutifully asked, "What?"

"You have to unwrap them."

"Yeah, most people agree they taste better that way."

He ignored my wisecrack. "That gets you involved. It gets you ready to hold them up to your mouth and bite into them. It prepares you for the wonderful taste of these things."

"Yeah. So what?"

"So, that's your next lesson."

"Eating Tastykakes?"

"Learning that a major part of comedy writing—of any writing, really—is preparing to write."

He took another bite of the coconut cake, but it was more for dramatic effect this time. He needed that pregnant pause. At the exact right time, he continued, "Suppose

I asked you right now to write ten jokes about television commercials. What would you do?"

"I don't know," I said.

"You'd start thinking of what commercials are on TV. Wouldn't you?"

"I guess I would. I'd need something to write about."

He said, "Of course, you would. That's research. You make a list of all the commercials you can think of. Now you have a whole bunch of commercials that you can write gags for. If you spend some time making that list, you'll find that you can write more quickly and you'll come up with more and better gags. That's called preparing to write. Make sense?"

"Makes sense."

He took another big bite of his cake as kind of a victory celebration, proud of himself for being so sagacious.

He said, "Now another part of this same idea is gathering references for your jokes."

I looked blank so he explained, "Most jokes are two ideas that are put together in a funny way. Take a joke like paying alimony is crazy. That's like buying a horse for somebody else to ride. You see, it's relating 'alimony' to 'having a horse you can't ride.' See?"

"Yeah, I do."

"How about a joke like this—'My date took me to a very secluded restaurant. It had to be secluded so the Board of Health couldn't find it.'"

"I get it. You're relating a terrible restaurant to a bad report from the Board of Health."

"Exactly. Now the more references you can find for a bad restaurant, the more gags you'll be able to generate. Right?"

"I guess so."

"Hey, once I tell you something, you don't have to guess anymore."

I held up my coffee cup in apology and said, "Sorry," then took a sip.

He went on. "Take your joke earlier about the skinny girl with no boobs. You can make a list of other things that could relate to the idea of skinny. She's built like a snake, she's the same shape as a stick, there's no room on her body for anything, she could go down the drain—stuff like that. You make a whole list of them before you get to the writing part. Then you'll find your writing becomes quicker and easier, and because of that...better."

"I'm sure it would."

He said, "Good. I got you out of the habit of guessing. I mean just right off the top of the head. 'This girl was so skinny, once she swallowed a walnut and six of her old boyfriends left town. She was so skinny, when she got a tattoo, it had to be continued on a friend.'"

I jumped in with a gag off the top of my head: "She was so skinny, she once went to a masquerade party wearing nothing but a white fuzzy hat and white fuzzy slippers—she was dressed as a Q-tip."

Bill said, "That's it. You get the idea."

"It's neat," I said. "I'm eager to try it."

"That's your homework for this week. Spend a little time preparing to write before you actually write. Do some research, gather some references, write all that stuff out before you begin to do the jokes."

"No problem," I said. I was looking forward to this assignment.

"And when you have a goal you want to achieve, you have to prepare for that, too."

"In what way? What do you mean?"

Bill had now started in on the blueberry pie. When he swallowed that first bite, his face looked more angelic than it ever had before.

Then he took a napkin from the dispenser, grabbed his felt-tip pen, and started to write as he answered my question. "If you're going to go on a trip somewhere in your car, you have to find out not only where you're going, but how you're going to get there."

"Right."

"So you need a roadmap, a . . ." Instead of finishing the sentence he held the napkin up for me to read.

I read aloud:

Prepare—have a plan of action

"Exactly," Bill said.

"Hold on now. I'm not the kind of guy who makes a lot of lists and figures out where he's going to be in two years, five years, ten years."

"I don't care if you make a list or not, but somewhere in your head you need a plan. It's like the joke about the airline pilot who announced to the passengers, 'I have good news and bad news. The bad news is that we're hopelessly lost. The good news is that we're making good time.'"

"That's an old joke."

"Hey, I'm not doing an act here; I'm trying to make a point. The point is—how do you know if you're making good time if you don't know where you're going?"

"I hate plans."

"Learn to love them. A good plan keeps you focused and we already discussed how important that is. It keeps you headed in the right direction. It says, 'I'm here right now; here's where I want to be sometime in the future.' It reminds you to keep going in that direction."

He paused for another bite of blueberry pie.

"A good plan allows you to see potential problems and avoid them. If you plan your car trip wisely, you may leave early in order to avoid the morning rush hour traffic in the city. Also a plan lets you measure and evaluate your progress. Is your career moving in the right direction and at the speed you'd like? If yes, fine. If no, what do you have to do to goose it along a bit?"

I emptied the carafe of coffee and signaled for more. Apparently this breakfast meeting still had some time left.

Bill went on. "A workable plan can help you break your project into bite-sized chunks. You're going to learn how that can help in your writing a little later; right now you're learning that it can be valuable in getting whatever it is you want."

"Bite-sized chunks?" I asked. "What am I going to do, eat my plan?"

"Smartass. Bite-sized chunks is just a figure of speech I used to get my point across. If you order a steak in a restaurant, you don't stuff the whole thing in your mouth, do you?"

"I don't, but you might."

"Smartass again. No, you cut it up into smaller pieces—bite-sized chunks. That's what you do with any project or goal. You don't try to do it all at once; you break it into smaller, doable projects—bite-sized chunks. I'm going to write that on your napkin." He added the words:

—in bite-sized chunks

and tossed the completed napkin to me.

The new pot of coffee arrived and I refilled Bill's cup and mine. As I tasted it, Bill went on about this precious plan.

"The plan can act as a source of encouragement while you're striving to achieve. Each small success, each chunk that is bitten off, goads you on to your next accomplishment. You know, like when you do a good show in a club, you're eager to write more jokes and get out there and do even better the next time."

Bill finished off the blueberry pie and washed the last mouthful down with a swallow of coffee. I looked at my watch; it was getting late. "And finally. . ."

"Oh good," I said, "You know I do have to get to work this morning."

"As I was saying. . . finally, a plan can get you started on your quest immediately. It's frustrating to keep wishing for something in the future. It's much more satisfying to be able to do something about it right now. As my old friend Lao Tzu is fond of saying, 'The journey of 1,000 miles begins with the first step.' With your plan you can not only guarantee that you'll take that first step, but that it will be in the right direction."

"Oh, so now you hang around with ancient Chinese philosophers?"

"Sure, God has made Heaven an equal-opportunity destination."

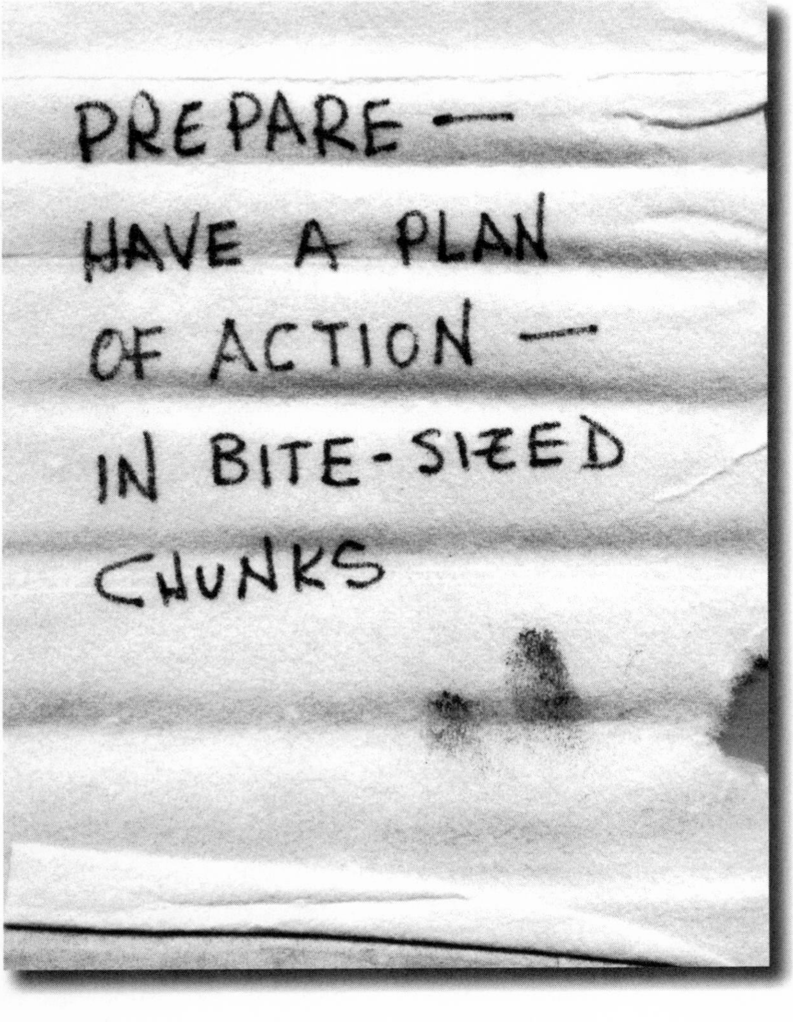
PREPARE —
HAVE A PLAN
OF ACTION —
IN BITE-SIZED
CHUNKS

"Wow," I answered raising my eyebrows in mock amazement. "Well, you can step down from your soapbox now."

"Not quite yet. The plan should be personalized. It should definitely be your plan. Not your agent's. Not your mom and dad's. Yours. It should be precise. Know what you want specifically. Some comic once said, 'I always wanted to be somebody. Maybe I should have been more specific.' Your outline should be well defined."

"Maybe I should be taking notes," I acknowledged.

Bill said, "Yes, you should be. The next thing to note is that your plan should be incremental. Remember, small, bite-sized chunks. Go from Point A to Point B, then from Point B to Point C. Don't try to swallow the whole megilla in one gulp."

"Like you did with those Tastykakes?"

He ignored my fabulous witticism. He seemed to have a tendency for that.

"Your plan should include only those things you can control. Have you heard of John Wooden?"

"Yeah, the legendary basketball coach at UCLA."

"The winningest coach in history. Yet, strangely enough, he never once during his coaching career mentioned winning to his players. He advised them to be prepared and to play their best. That was something they could control. Winning was not."

I had to leave if I was going to make it to work on time. "Listen, this was some lesson," I said. "I've got a lot of writing, thinking, and planning to do."

"Yes, you do if you want to get a diploma from my school. We'll get together next week. Same time, same place."

He called the waitress over. "Can you put these in a doggie bag to go? My schnauzer loves apple pie and lemon pie." She left to get the bag.

I said, "You don't have a dog."

"I don't? You think angels don't have pets?"

"You're not a guardian angel, Bill."

"You know I really shouldn't care whether you believe in guardian angels or not. But I'm starting to get a little ticked off with your lack of faith."

"Oh, c'mon, you don't still expect me to buy this angel baloney do you?"

The waitress brought him a small bag and laid the check face down on the table. He picked up the bag and put the pies into it. He said, "Normally, we're not permitted to do what I'm going to do, but you've got me so pissed off I'm going to try to get away with it. I think I can sneak this one by God."

"I thought God sees all things," I said.

"He used to, but He's getting old."

"How many times have you been struck by lightning?" I asked.

"Ye of little faith, I'm going to give you proof. Before we meet next week, I, as your guardian angel, will have saved you from serious harm. How's that for proof?"

"Yeah, sure," I said with a dismissive shake of the hand. "I've got to get to work."

Bill said, "Hey, it's your turn to pick up the check. If I remember correctly, last week was my treat."

This guy was too damn much.

I picked up the breakfast tab and headed for the cashier.

CHAPTER ELEVEN...

I HONESTLY COULDN'T FIGURE THIS GUY, BILL, OUT. HE SEEMED to know what he was talking about. I tried all the suggestions he offered and they worked. They helped me turn out material and that helped my act. His non-writing advice was working for me also. I had a different attitude, a more positive approach to my career. For instance, I'd put together a plan and was following it. I was doing better than I ever had before. Things were starting to happen. I even had a big gig in the works—that agent I told you about was negotiating it for me. I didn't talk to anyone about it in fear it might jinx the whole shebang.

Now, whether any of that had anything to do with Bill or not, I don't know. It's like when you take some sort of medicine to cure whatever ails you and you get better. You don't really know if the medicine worked or if whatever was bothering you just ran its course.

Still, Bill was always on my mind. He was kind of like a song you hear on the radio and then you keep humming it to yourself over and over again until another song replaces it. Maybe that's what I had to do to get him out of my head—wait for another guy to come along and claim to be my guardian angel.

That messenger from Heaven story was pure bunk. I dismissed that the first time he bummed a drink off me. He was no guardian angel, but I couldn't figure out his racket. See, that's the thing that kept eating at me. There must be something in this for him. Something more than a few meals.

I was sure he was harmless enough. I didn't think he was up to any serious mischief but he must have had some angle. If not, he was going to a lot of trouble for what? The fun of it? And yet I kept on with the breakfasts and the lessons. Why? Well, as I said, they were helping me. Or at least, I thought they were. And he was a charming guy in an obnoxious sort of way. He was funny. I liked the give and take with him. It kind of sharpened my funny bone.

But why was I letting him take charge of me? I mean, whatever he said to do, I did. Normally, I'm a stubborn, cynical, arrogant kind of guy. If somebody tells me to do something, that's plenty of reason for me not to do it. Yet when Bill told me to do this or do that, what did I do? I did this or I did that. Did he really have some sort of mystic, supernatural power over me?

These are the kind of things I was thinking of as I was winding up my work week. I had my last delivery of the day to make to Rohn's Drug Store. I made deliveries to Rohn's several times a week, but I always liked to make it my last stop at the end of the week. It was close to the supply company. I could deliver the supplies, drop the truck off at the parking lot, and head home to relax for awhile and start going over my material for my weekend performances.

I was thinking about Bill, though, instead of thinking about my job. I drove right by my turn. It was a turn I had made hundreds of times before. In fact, if I felt like taking a nap, I could doze off and the truck would drive to Rohn's Drug Store on its own. Today, though, I drove right past Rohn's street.

Because of the one-way streets in that part of town, I had to go several blocks out of my way, circle around, and come back to make the delivery. Of course, it was the end of the day so there was lots of traffic on each of the streets I had to take. Normally, I'm pretty calm in city traffic—I cope with it every day as part of the job—but this was on my time now and I was pissed.

When I reached Rohn's, there were red and blue lights flashing, crowds gathered, and no way I could stop to make my delivery. As I passed by the policemen redirecting traffic, I could see what the problem was. An SUV was rammed into the side of Rohn's wall. Apparently, it had gone out of control, jumped the curb, and slammed into the building right where I normally parked my delivery truck.

I thought to myself, if I had been here earlier...if I hadn't gone past my turn...if I hadn't had to drive around several blocks...I might have been in the truck and crunched by that SUV.

Bill said he would save me from serious harm this week.

Was this guy really my guardian angel?

Couldn't be.

No way.

But then again....

CHAPTER TWELVE...

I WAS REALLY EAGER FOR THE NEXT MONDAY BREAKFAST meeting with Bill. It was confrontation time. I was going to find out once and for all who he was, where he came from, what his scam was, what he knew about my close call at Rohn's on Friday, how he knew about it, and what, if anything, he had to do with it.

I marched into that coffee shop like David must have strutted out to meet Goliath. I would even deliver a sling shot to Bill's head if I had to, but I was going to get answers.

Bill hadn't arrived yet, so I slid into the booth that we had occupied these past few Monday mornings. The waitress came over and I quickly ordered hot, black coffee.

She didn't bother taking out her pad. She said, "You're here to meet with your friend."

"He may not be my friend after today," I said.

"They just took him away in an ambulance."

"What?" I stammered. "What happened?"

She said, "I don't know. He was sitting here having coffee and he just kind of slumped over in the booth. I didn't know what to do, so I called 911."

"And they took him away?"

"Yeah, it was terrible."

"Where did they take him? Do you know?"

She said, "I'm not sure, but I think they generally take emergencies to St. Agnes's. It's the closest."

As I rushed toward the door she shouted after me, "He never paid for his coffee."

I turned, handed her two bucks, and said, "He never does."

Then I dashed out and headed for St. Ag's.

CHAPTER THIRTEEN...

THERE WAS AN AMBULANCE RIGHT OUTSIDE THE EMERGENCY entrance of St. Agnes's Hospital with the back doors open as if they had just arrived and wheeled someone in quickly. Of course, there's probably an ambulance parked outside of practically every emergency room entrance in the nation. Still, I took this as a positive sign that Bill was inside. I pulled into one of the "Emergency Only" spots.

Who should I ask about once I got inside the building, though? Bill never told me his last name. Was Bill his real first name? I didn't even know that for sure. I could kick myself for spending so much time with this guy and never even asking for his last name.

The only thing he did let me know about himself was that he liked to eat and drink and didn't like to pay. He was also cocky as hell, but I doubted if any of that would be on the admittance forms.

Standing in the emergency waiting room, I tried to look inconspicuous and observe the chaotic action. Nurses and receptionists were busy with a mother and her infant who was screaming inconsolably. A teenager holding a bandage over some sort of wound on his right hand sat with a few of his friends complaining about how long it was taking to get any attention.

The hospital personnel, seemingly indifferent to the suffering about them, walked around with their clipboards handing out documents instead of medication, constantly repeating the mantra of most hospitals—"fill this out, fill this out, fill this out."

Trying to look like I knew what I was doing, I marched past the pandemonium and through the double swinging doors that led to the emergency room inner sanctum. My ploy worked. Of course, being in show business I was used to going backstage. I got into where the sick and wounded were being treated rather than simply interrogated.

Luck was with me. Bill was in the second cubicle I peeked into. He had tubes or wires coming from his fingers, his arms, his nose, and was hooked up to monitors that clicked and beeped information that meant something to somebody, but not to me. Other than that, Bill looked pretty good. He was awake and alert. He recognized me.

"You look like hell," he said.

"What do you expect from a guy who has just seen his guardian angel lying half-naked on a gurney with tubes coming out of every part of him?"

"Yeah, when God told me to take the form of a human body, I should have picked one that had a better warranty."

"What happened?" I asked.

"I don't know," he said. "I went to the diner to meet you. I was there. Then I was here."

A nurse who looked like she worked days at the hospital and nights for the World Wrestling Federation came in and said to me, "What are you doing in here?"

"I'm family," I lied.

She said, "I don't care who you are. You're not supposed to be in here. You wait in the waiting room and we'll keep you informed."

"But I want to know how he's doing," I said.

"We don't know how he's doing yet," a pleasanter voice behind me said. It was a young doctor who came into the cubicle after I did.

I turned to face the doctor. He seemed friendlier than Attila-the-Nurse so I asked him, "Is he going to be okay?"

The doctor held out his hand in greeting and said, "Doctor John Petty."

I shook his hand and said, "Chuck Barry. I'm a friend."

The nurse interrupted. "I thought you said you were family."

"I'm also a liar."

The doctor calmly told me, "We won't know how he's doing until we have a better look at him."

"You have to get out of here," the militant nurse insisted.

The doctor was more reasonable. He said, "I can't tell you much right now, but we're definitely going to admit him. Why don't you go home, come back later, and we'll be able to tell you much more then."

Then a huge cop came in and said, "If that's your car in the emergency spot, you're going to have to move it... right now."

"It said 'emergency' and I considered this an emergency so I thought I was entitled...."

The cop repeated, "Right now."

Bill said, "Kid. I'll be here awhile. Go move your car, go to work, and come back and see me tonight."

The cop apparently agreed with Bill and grabbed my arm. "Let's go," he said.

As he was leading me out, Bill called to me. "Chuck."

I turned.

"When you come tonight...bring some soft pretzels with you."

I looked towards the doctor who was reading something on the clipboard. He gave me a look and a shrug that I took to mean that soft pretzels would do no harm.

As I let the cop lead me out, Bill hollered, "With mustard."

CHAPTER FOURTEEN...

THE CUSTOMERS GOT WHIRLWIND SERVICE THAT DAY. ANXIOUS to get back to St. Ag's to see how Bill was doing and what exactly was wrong with him, I rushed through all my deliveries. I drove and worked carefully, though. After all, my guardian angel was on the disabled list. I was either left totally unprotected or I was saddled with a second stringer.

Oh, as I said, I knew that Bill wasn't really my guardian angel. It's just that he was so dedicated to this charade of his that some little part of my brain sort of half believed it. Besides, I realized for the first time that I was sort of enjoying playing along with him.

But on my way to the hospital at the end of my workday, it dawned on me that I still didn't know who I was going to ask for. Sure, Bill and I'd been schmoozing and I had been following his dictates for a couple of months now, yet I knew nothing about him. We always met either in the clubs or in the diner, so I didn't know where he lived. He never told me what he does or used to do for a living. His last name was a mystery. I kind of felt like some of my buddies who would meet a girl in the club, have a few drinks with her, take her home or to a motel, say goodbye the next morning, and part company without ever learning her last name. Many times, not learning even her first name.

It left me with a guilty feeling. Bill and I were like a one-night stand.

To me he was, as the song said, "Just plain Bill." Either that, or in our kidding way, he was Archangel Shecky. No way I could go up to the hospital receptionist and ask, "Do you have an Archangel Shecky here?" They'd slap me into the psycho ward. And regardless how many beds St. Agnes's Hospital had, it's a good bet that more than a few of them were occupied by guys named Bill.

My only option was to start where I started this morning—in the emergency room. Who knows what I expected to find. Maybe Bill left a trail of crumbs leading to his room. That was obviously wishful thinking because the way Bill ate, he didn't leave crumbs.

Luck was with me again—or maybe my real guardian angel was. The nurse I'd tangled with earlier—the one who had me thrown out—was the first person I ran into in the emergency waiting room.

"Hi. Do you remember me?" I said.

"You're not going to cause trouble again?"

"No," I said, "I'm just trying to find my good friend who was in here this morning."

"Well, he's certainly not in here now."

"I figured that," I told her. "I'm just trying to find him."

"Look, I'm very busy. Ask upstairs at the reception desk."

"Well, I can't really. I don't know his last name."

She eyed me suspiciously. "You must be very close friends."

She obviously didn't have time to listen to my explanation and she wouldn't have believed it anyway, so I just said, "It's a long story."

She said, "I don't have time for long or short stories," and tried to maneuver past me.

"Please," I said, "I don't know where else to go. If I could just find out his name or what room he's in."

She looked at me and that militant expression softened—just a bit. "Come on."

She led me to the emergency room reception desk, fiddled through a few papers, found what she was searching for, and said, "His name's William Shaughnessy. He's probably been admitted. You can ask for his room number at the main entrance."

"What's wrong with him?" I asked.

"I can't give you that information. You'll have to talk to him or his doctor about that."

"Thank you, so much," I said. "I don't know how to repay you."

She must have smelled the soft pretzels in the bag I was carrying. "Are those fresh pretzels in the bag?"

"Would you like one?"

"I'd love one. I haven't had a bite to eat since you were in here this morning. This place has been a madhouse."

I broke three of the pretzels off and handed them to her. She immediately bit into one and rushed off to her many crises in the ER. Before going through the swinging doors she turned to me and said through a mouthful of half-eaten pretzel, "The next time you rush a friend to the hospital, learn his last name."

The receptionist seated behind the desk looked at me pleadingly. I broke off another cluster of pretzels and handed those to her before I started upstairs to find Bill.

CHAPTER FIFTEEN...

WHEN I MARCHED INTO ROOM 276, WHERE THEY HAD SETTLED Bill, I had a lot of questions I wanted answered. First among them, how Bill was doing and what sort of problem he had that required hospitalization. He looked fairly comfortable and not all that ill, but he must have been, I figured, or he wouldn't be here. However, I also wanted to know who he was, what his gambit was, why did he pick me, and a few other questions that would probably pop into my head during my visit. Bill wanted to know only one thing.

"Did you bring the pretzels?"

"I did." I held the bag up in front of me, teasing Bill.

"And the mustard?" he asked.

"You're not going to get one single soft pretzel until I get some answers."

"You're holding my pretzels hostage?"

I said, "They're my pretzels. I paid for them. I'm in charge of them. I'll give them to you when I'm good and ready and I won't be good and ready until I get some answers from you—some truthful answers."

He pleaded. "Come on. I'm starving to death here."

"You've got a whole tray of good food right next to your bed."

"That's not food. It's hospital stuff."

He held up the small dish of gelatin. "Look at this. Have you ever seen such a hideous color in your life?"

It was an alarming shade of green. It looked even more insidious when it jiggled slightly.

Bill said, "Anything this color is not made to be eaten. It's made to frighten vampires away. Give me a pretzel, please."

I handed him the bag of pretzels because the hospital food did look horrifyingly inedible.

"But I still want answers," I said.

"You'll get them," he promised. "Right after I have a taste of these beauties."

Peering into the bag, Bill gave me a quizzical look. "The payment's a little light, isn't it?"

I told him I had to bribe some of the hospital staff.

Obviously he wasn't happy with the quantity of pretzels, but he was eager to chomp down on what was there.

He opened the small mustard jar and used the straw from his water container to spread the condiment liberally on one of the pretzels. He bit into it, chewed, swallowed, and sighed ecstatically, "Pretty damned delicious."

He took another bite.

"You got your pretzels," I reminded him. "I want my answers."

"Okay, here's the story," he mumbled between bites.

"The true story," I interjected.

"The true story," he conceded.

He chewed a bit before he continued. "My name is William Shaughnessy. Have you ever heard of me?"

"Why would I have heard of you?"

"I'll get into that later," Bill said. "I was born and raised right here in South Philly."

"So you have tasted sticky buns, hoagies, cheese steaks, Tastykakes..."

"Of course," he said. "I've been eating them all my life."

"You're a fraud, you know that?"

"Always have been," he said casually. "Now do you want to hear the story or not?"

"Go ahead."

"I was educated in the Catholic Schools. When I graduated high school—Bishop Neumann—I went right into the Seminary—St. Charles Barromeo. You heard of it?"

"Sure I heard of it. You were going to be a priest? Were you that religious back then?"

He said, "No, of course not. Strangely enough, it wasn't really a religious thing. It was more like show business."

That threw me. "Show business? How do you get that?"

"Well," he said, "Religious people were special. Heck, the nuns would get into the Phillies games for free. Priests could get discounts at everything. People treated you different. It was instant respect. People looked up to you, like they do at celebrities."

"So you were going to be a priest because it was easier than being a movie star."

He shrugged. "It wasn't easier, especially not for me. The other seminarians read *The Lives of the Saints*, *The Following of Christ*, and all those other religious books. Me? I read the lives of show business stars."

"Really?"

"Yeah, really. During our spiritual reading periods I read Bing Crosby's autobiography, *Call Me Lucky*. Bob Hope had one, too, called *Have Tux, Will Travel*. I read them all. I wasn't interested in saints; I was fascinated with stars."

"So I take it you didn't last too long in the seminary."

He smeared another pretzel with mustard, took a bite and went on, "No, I was too interested in show business to waste my time being holy. But the world did miss out on some pretty entertaining homilies, I'll tell you that."

"You sounded like Bob Hope when you said that."

Bill agreed. "Yeah, I loved Hope's style."

I said, "So, you went to be a priest, but you didn't become a priest. So how does that bring us here tonight?"

"I'm getting to that. Would you let me tell the story? Damn, there's only two of us in the room and I get a heckler."

"Sorry," I said.

"So anyway, I read a book about Danny Thomas. Have you heard of him?"

"Of course I have."

"Well, Danny was having a rough time making it as an entertainer. You know that feeling."

Bill never passed up an opportunity to get a dig in.

He went on. "So this book said he went into a church one day and said a prayer to St. Jude. He's the patron saint of hopeless cases, you know."

"I think I did know that. I might have to call on him for my act."

Bill said, "No, you won't. You've got me."

"And how exactly did I get you?"

"I'm coming to that. You're heckling again."

I settled into a more comfortable position in the chair—a position that said I'm prepared to sit here now and just listen.

Bill continued, "So, Danny Thomas promised St. Jude that day that if Jude would help him make it in show business he would repay him by helping all of mankind. He would use whatever success and wealth he gained to benefit other people who were 'hopeless cases.' Well, as you know, Danny Thomas became a major star...and..." Bill held up his finger here to emphasize the importance of this next statement, "He did establish the St. Jude's hospital for Children."

"I know. He was a great man."

Bill said, "Well, I figured if it was good enough for Danny Thomas, it was good enough for Bill Shaughnessy. So I went into the chapel at St. Charles seminary and I made the same kind of promise. I told St. Charles that if he could get me out of this dumb seminary and into a show business career, I would do good for people, too."

"Like what kind of good?" I asked.

"I didn't know at the time. It was just bravado. Make me a star now and send me a bill later. I'd do something, but I didn't know what."

"And St. Charles fell for this, huh?"

"I guess he did," Bill replied. "I got out of the seminary and I did get into show business. And things went pretty well. I wrote lots of jokes and people started to buy them. I went out to Hollywood and got hot. I wrote for Bob Hope and Lucille Ball, and many top notch TV shows and legendary stand-up performers. I was the guy performers went to when they wanted good, solid, funny material. That's why I thought you might have heard of me."

I said, "I'm sensing there's a big 'but' that goes with this story."

Bill said, "Yes there is. I was hot, I was having fun, I was making money...but...then I lost it."

"What? The scotch? Drugs? What?"

"No, nothing like that. I didn't destroy my life. I just let it kind of slip silently away. I had a wife and a young boy, but I wasn't much of a husband or father. Then one day they just up and left. I don't really know what happened. I haven't seen my son since. I have a granddaughter somewhere but I've never seen her. I don't even know her name. It's kind of sad." Then, trying to break himself out of the self-sympathy mode, he added with fake cheerfulness, "But hey, I brought it all on myself."

I asked, "Are you in trouble now? Do you need money or anything like that?"

"No. I'm fine. I got my pension and my health insurance. The people in show business take pretty good care of their own."

"But you are in the hospital. So what's the problem?" I asked.

Bill didn't respond right away. This question had obviously touched a nerve. Almost reluctantly, he continued with his tale. "Not too long ago I got some pretty scary health news."

"Was that when you were gone for those three or four weeks?" I asked.

"Yeah, they did some tests and they didn't turn out too good."

"What's the problem?"

"That's not important."

"It is to me. What's wrong with you?"

"You don't really have to know, but okay. I've got a rare disease."

"Like what?"

"It's called Antimacassar Syndrome."

"What?"

He said, "I told you it was rare. Antimacassar—A-N-T-I-M-A-C-A-S-S-A-R."

I jotted this down because I was determined to find out how serious Bill's ailment really was. When I'd finished writing I asked, "What is it?"

Bill barked, "Do you want to be a doctor or do you want to be a comedian? I can only teach one thing at a time."

"Okay...okay...sorry."

"Anyway," Bill went on, "this got me to thinking. St. Charles did his part. I made it in show business, I made some money, I made a name for myself. Things were good. But I never kept my part of the bargain. Danny Thomas did wonderful things with his good fortune; I did nothing. I not only didn't do any good for the world, I didn't even do much good for my own family. So, when I got the scary news I decided now was the time to live up to my part of the contract. I would try to help somebody who wanted to make it in show business—in comedy, which is the only thing I know anything about."

"And that's where I come in."

"That's where you come in," Bill said. "I figured if I helped even one person, that person might be able to help some other people. It was kind of like I was paying off my promise on the installment plan."

"But why me?"

This question must have shook Bill up because he reached over to the food tray, grabbed the vampire-green gelatin, and started to eat it. This must have been his dessert since the pretzels were gone. After the first swallow he said, "This stuff is pretty damn awful." But he kept eating anyway.

I reminded him. "I asked why you picked me."

Bill said, "That, I think, was divine inspiration."

"How?"

"Well," he explained. "Your name is Chuck, which is short for Charles. You know, like St. Charles Barromeo. And your last name is Barry which is like a short form of Barromeo, like in St. Charles Barromeo."

"That's the dumbest divine inspiration I've ever heard. The Chuck part makes a little bit of sense, but the saint's name is St. Charles Borromeo, not Barromeo."

"Is it really?" Bill asked.

"It is," I said.

He thought about that, then said, "So what? Just be glad I didn't go to the church of Sts. Felicitas and Perpetua to make the promise. Anyway, I went to a few comedy clubs and I liked your style. You do the kind of jokes that I can write—the kind of comedy writing that I can teach. So that's how I decided to become your guardian angel."

All I could say was, "Wow."

"Was it worth a few drinks and a bagful of soft pretzels?"

Almost on cue, a nurse came in to collect his dishes, most of them still filled with food. She said, "You didn't eat much, Mr. Shaughnessy."

"No, just a little bit of the gelatin,"

"Did you enjoy it?"

"It was delicious," he lied.

"Yeah," she said, "That's my favorite, too. I just love that color."

She exited with the tray.

I still had questions. "Tell me something, though."

Bill said, "Yeah?"

"Why did you pull the whole guardian angel bit?"

Bill said, "To get your attention, man."

"You got it all right. I thought you were a nutcake."

"Yeah, but you listened to me, right?"

"If you had just told me that you were a comedy writer who was trying to help me out with my act, I would have listened to you more than I would a guy who thinks he's my guardian angel."

Bill chuckled at my logic. "Do you really believe that?"

"Sure I do," I said. "Who's going to listen to a crackpot who thinks he's a guardian angel?"

"You."

"Yeah, but I was just playing along with you. If you had told me who you wrote jokes for, I would have really listened."

Bill shot up in bed when I said that. This seemed to be a point he really wanted to discuss and I was getting afraid that maybe this kind of chatter was not really good for him in his condition.

"You would not have," he said. "And I'll tell you why."

"Oh, now we're back to the guardian angel who sees all things and knows all things."

"No, I don't know all things, but I do know this—you youngsters in comedy today think that you're the hippest and the sharpest that ever walked into a spotlight. You think the guys I worked for—the Henny Youngmans, the Milton Berles, the Red Skeltons—they were all old-fashioned fuddy duddies."

"Fuddy duddies?"

"See. You even make fun of our language. You guys are so hip and cool that you don't even listen to the old masters or the guys, like me, who wrote for them."

I had to defend my colleagues. "You guys don't know what's happening today."

"And you guys don't know what happened yesterday, but you should. Many of today's comics are smart and clever and hilarious, but they can still learn from those comedians who went before them."

"Why do you ancient guys always think the older comics were better?"

"I didn't say they were better; I said you could learn from them . . . and you can. Those guys were hip enough to climb out of the pack and become big stars. Wouldn't you like to know how to do that?"

"Sure," I said.

"They were sharp enough to keep their careers alive for decades. A lot of today's youngsters would sure like to know how to do that. Sure, these guys were from a different time, but they knew how to play their audiences. They were determined, dedicated, and funny. That's how they became big stars. Don't you think there's a lesson to be learned from that?"

"I guess there is."

"How many times do I have to tell you, when I tell you something, you don't have to guess anymore. And these legendary performers lasted because they knew what they were doing and they knew their audiences—the audiences of their time."

I said, "I believe all that. I don't know what you're getting so upset about. You'd better take it easy. You're in a hospital, for crying out loud."

Bill wouldn't be calmed. "You believe it now but you wouldn't have believed it just because some old guy who used to write jokes told it to you. No, you would have considered me an old-fart has-been. So that's why I became your guardian angel."

I said, "Geez, I had no idea this was a major production on your part."

"Well, it was. It was show business, kid. It was pizzazz. It was flair."

"Damn, you're proud of yourself, aren't you?"

"I sure am," Bill said. "Besides, it gave me a character to play. And that's another thing you can learn from the old-timers while we're on the subject."

"Bill, I don't think we were on that subject any longer."

"Well, we are," he said. "You can learn how important it is to have a strong stage persona. The character you play at the microphone is important. It was easy to write stingy jokes for Jack Benny because he developed that character. George Burns milked his longevity for every possible joke imaginable. Phyllis Diller turned her funny looks and her face lifts into a comedy gold mine. And their jokes worked because the character they presented was so strong, so larger than life. And you say you have nothing to learn from the old-timers."

"I didn't say that, Bill. You did."

"But you and your cronies think it. And I'm telling you, for the good of your careers, it's time to rethink it."

Bill got himself so worked up about this that he grabbed for the water cup by his bedside and took a drink. He made a terrible face when he swallowed. "Damn, this stuff tastes like wet mustard."

I had no idea what wet mustard tasted like, but it must be awful. I took the straw from his drinking cup, rinsed it out in the faucet, and returned it to him. He sipped the water again.

"That's much better," he said. Then back to the subject. "And another reason I went with the guardian angel bit was because it was fun for me. I enjoyed it."

I said, "Well, I'm happy for you."

"Because, basically," he said, "you're a rather dull guy."

"Okay," I said. "That does it. I'm outta here. I'm going to go home and get some rest. I have to get up and go to work in the morning. And you get yourself a good sleep. You have to get up in the morning and do whatever you have to do to get over this..." I reached into my pocket and pulled out the slip of paper I had written his ailment on. I read it. "...Antimacassar Syndrome, whatever the hell that is."

Then I remembered the problem that had been bothering me. I had to ask about it. "Tell me one thing, though. How did you know that you would protect me from an injury last week?"

Bill laughed heartily. "I protected you from injury? How? What happened?"

I told him about the incident outside of Rohn's drug store—how it was a terrible accident and I would have been involved if I hadn't missed my street.

He laughed harder.

I said, "You find it funny that I almost got killed?"

"You didn't almost get killed. You were nowhere near the accident."

"But I could have been and should have been. So did you save me or not?"

"I had nothing to do with it," Bill said. "That's an old fortune teller's trick. You tell somebody something, anything, and they'll find some way to make it come true or seem to come true."

"You're a real jerk," I said.

"Me? You're the jerk that fell for it."

I headed for the door and said, "I'll come back and see you again."

Bill said, "Aren't you forgetting something?"

I said, "I'm not going to kiss you goodbye."

He said, "You're still enrolled in the Archangel Shecky School of Comedy and Get What You Want-iveness. You're not getting out of here without a comedy assignment."

I said, "You're sick. Take some time off."

"I'm sick, so we have to work faster."

"No, you get some rest."

"Sit down," Bill demanded. "This'll only take a minute and I got all the time in the world to sleep. I got a bed under me twenty-four hours a day."

I figured it would be easier to give in and get it over with than it would be to get him worked up with another argument. I sat down and listened.

Bill said, "You've been writing faithfully every week, right?"

"I have."

"I know you have. I know all things, remember?"

"No, you don't."

"Doesn't matter. So long as I think I do."

"You know something? I think you're starting to believe you're an angel now."

Bill did his ignoring me thing again and continued. "All right, listen. I want you to do more than write jokes this week. I want you to tell a story."

I was confused. "What do you mean?"

"I mean," Bill said, "that I want you to write a full monologue. Do maybe twenty-five to thirty-five jokes all about one topic. Put the jokes in a logical order and make it conversational—like you're just talking off the top of your head to this one audience."

"Okay," I said. "I can do that."

"And make the gags consistent. You know what I mean? Don't do one joke early in the routine and then contradict it later in the routine. Everything has to be consistent, it has to flow."

"I got you." I said.

"That takes care of the writing. Now to the 'Get What You Want-iveness' part of your matriculation."

"You're one tough teacher, you know that?"

"You got that right. And I want you to be one tough professional comedian."

"What do you mean?"

"When you're going after a goal, you have to start out with the right attitude."

"Which is?"

"Well, now, that depends on what you're going after. A boxer has to decide that he's not afraid to take a few punches to the face."

"I'm not going to be a boxer."

"Good, so you won't need a cut man. A writer has to get used to the fact that rejection is part of that profession. Manuscripts will be rejected; well written articles will be edited. Publishers will want this chapter removed and another chapter rewritten. A writer has to be prepared for that."

"I'm not going to be a writer, either."

"You're going to have nights when the jokes don't work. The audience will just sit there. You're going to have agents that won't handle you and club owners that won't book you. You're going to write great jokes and the audience will hear them and just stare."

"That's a tough life you're painting for me."

"It's not just you. It's not just comedians. No matter what profession you go into, you're going to get kicked in the teeth every so often. If you're ready for it, you'll shake it off quicker and keep moving towards your goal."

"Again, Bill, you make it sound easy."

"It's not. But now, at the beginning, is the time to analyze whatever goal you're pursuing, figure out what some of the obstacles will be—and you'll hit them, believe me—and develop a tenacious, failure-is-not-an-option attitude so you can deal with them."

"I got it."

"Yeah, but you'll need a reminder. Hand me a napkin there, will you."

I said, "Bill, I don't need a napkin. I understand."

"You're going to get one anyway."

I took a napkin that was left on his bedside table and handed it to him. He wrote:

Be prepared for setbacks. Develop a failure-is-not-an-option attitude

and held it out to me.

After I read it, I said, "It makes sense, Bill." And I wasn't just saying that. It really did make sense.

He said, "Okay, now get out of here and let me get some rest before they wake me up to give me my sleeping pill."

"That's an old joke."

"It's not a joke," Bill said. "They actually do that."

"I'll see you tomorrow night, then."

"No, you won't."

"Yeah, I'll stop by after work."

"No. You've got enough homework to do without wasting your time visiting the sick and wounded."

"I want to."

"I don't want you to. We agreed to meet once a week and that's what we'll do. I'll see you next Monday after work."

"All right."

"Bring your homework with you."

"I will."

"And some food."

I said, "Okay, what kind of food do you want me to bring you on my next visit?"

"Surprise me."

"Maybe I'll bring you something healthy."

"I said 'surprise me' not 'kill me.'"

"Goodnight, Shecky," I said and left.

BE PREPARED FOR
SETBACKS. DEVELOP A
FAILURE-IS-NOT-AN-OPTION
ATTITUDE

CHAPTER SIXTEEN...

It was only Wednesday, but I stopped in to visit with Bill anyway. I knew I was breaking Archangel Shecky's rules, but I had a problem I wanted him to help me with. He wasn't really surprised when I showed up because when I walked in he pointed his finger at me and shouted, "Aha! I knew you couldn't wait till Monday."

"Well, you're right again, Archangel Shecky."

"I'm always right. You should have learned that by now. And furthermore, I know exactly why you're here."

"Oh, Great-Learned-One, and why is that?"

"It's because you're having trouble with that assignment I gave you."

I said, "No...."

He didn't let me finish. "C'mon, own up to it. You're having trouble with it."

He was right; it wasn't an easy assignment. I said, "Okay, I am having trouble, but that's not..."

"You know why you're having trouble?"

"I'm sure you'll tell me."

"I will tell you. I know you're having trouble because that assignment I gave you is just about impossible."

"Were you trying to torment me? Why would you give me something to do that's impossible?"

He pretended not to hear me.

"It's practically impossible to write twenty-five or thirty-five gags on one subject, isn't it?"

"Yeah." I decided to say as little as I could so he could ramble on and get whatever he was going to say anyway out of his system.

"But I'll bet you can easily come up with five or six lines on one topic, right?"

"Right," I said.

"So here's Archangel Shecky's little trick to help you write twenty-five to thirty-five jokes on a topic."

"Which you said was impossible." I was trying to taunt him a bit, but again he ignored me.

"You divide your topic into five or six subtopics. Remember we talked about this before—bite-sized chunks. If you're writing about rush hour traffic, you might write a few jokes about how heavy the traffic is. Then you write a few on how close the cars are jammed together. Another subtopic might be how angry people get in this traffic. The next subtopic could be how these people show their anger. Different ways you might try to avoid the traffic. Then maybe you finish up with how relaxed you feel when you finally get out of traffic. Does all that make sense?"

"Yeah, it does."

"Okay, then you write five or six jokes on each subtopic and when you're done, you've got a whole routine written about one topic, namely heavy traffic."

"Okay, Bill," I said, "I'll try that. But first I have something I want to ask you . . ."

"No, let me ask you something first."

"Okay."

"Did you bring any food with you?"

"No, I was just going to make this a quick visit and I wasn't thinking about food."

"How can anyone live in Philadelphia and not think about food? Oh well, go ahead. What did you want to ask?"

"I have a problem, Bill, and I need your help."

"Keep going."

"You know, things have been going much better with my act lately."

"Doesn't sound like a problem."

I went on. "And an agent has been promising me some better work."

"Still doesn't sound like a problem."

"Well, he finally closed the deal and he called offering me a traveling gig as a comedian on a cruise ship. It starts out with a four week cruise, but if I do well, there's a good chance it could lead to a much longer gig—on different ships to different places, you know."

"And you're afraid to take the job."

He was right again. "Well, I'm a little scared, you know. It means I'd have to give up my truck driving job and I don't have anything else lined up."

"So taking this gig means that you'd be totally committed to your comedy career."

"That's right."

"And without a safety net, right?"

"Yeah, because I'd be giving up my day job."

"So, let me get this straight. This job could be the start of something big—Chuck Barry, famous comedian."

"It could be. Yeah."

"But it also could be the end of everything, right?"

"That's what I'm afraid of. That's why I came here to ask you what I should do."

"I see," he said. Then he appeared perplexed—like he was thinking this problem through. "This is a tough one," he said. "You should have brought food."

"I'm sorry," I said. "I didn't think."

"You know what this means, don't you?"

"No, I don't."

"Well, you've been studying at Archangel Shecky's School of Comedy and Get What You Want-iveness for some time now. You've been doing well. This, I think, is your final exam."

"I don't follow you, Bill."

He said, "You've really wanted to make it as a comedian."

"Pretty near all my life," I said.

"You've studied and you've worked hard at it."

"I busted my tail."

He said, "Well, it always comes to this—the final exam. The moment when you pass or fail."

"I still don't follow you."

"Anytime anyone pursues a goal—any goal, not just comedy—there comes that moment when you have to take a risk. If you want to be a skydiver, there's that moment when you have to step out of the plane. If you write a novel, you have to submit it to an agent or a publisher who may reject it. If you watch those poker games on TV, there comes a time when one of them has to say, 'I'm all in.' You've come to that point, Chuck."

"You've nailed it, Bill, but I don't know what to do."

"So you want Archangel Shecky to decide."

"That's why I came here tonight."

"This is a very tough decision."

"I know it is."

"I need some time to think about it."

"But I don't have time. The agent needs an answer ASAP."

He just went on as if I hadn't said anything. "You know what else I need? I need a hoagie."

"What?"

"I need a hoagie. It'll help me think."

"I'm not getting you a hoagie now. They have food here in the hospital. Ask the nurse for a snack."

"They don't have food in the hospital. They have wet sawdust that's shaped like food. Go out and get me a hoagie and when you come back, I'll have your answer for you."

"Where am I going to get a hoagie now?"

"You take the elevator down to the first floor. You go out the main lobby entrance, you turn right, you walk thirty-seven steps, you stop, you look around, and right there will be a great hoagie shop."

"You're crazy."

"No, I'm not. In Philadelphia, you take thirty-seven steps in any direction, stop, look around, and you'll be near a great hoagie shop." Bill started to look a little distracted.

I asked him, "Are you all right?"

"Yeah, I'm fine," he said. "Get a hoagie for yourself and one for me. We can have them while we're discussing your problem."

"Are you sure you're all right? You don't look so good."

"I'm hungry, for crying out loud. You come visiting somebody in a hospital and you don't bring food, what do you expect? Go get me a hoagie."

There was no arguing when Bill got his mind set, so I left him to think, and maybe rest a bit, while I walked those thirty-seven steps to great hoagies.

CHAPTER SEVENTEEN...

WHEN I—AND THE HOAGIES—RETURNED AND REACHED THE corridor that led to Bill's room, my heart started racing. Something was wrong. Bill's door was closed and three doctors were standing outside it having a serious, ominous discussion. I raced to them, interrupted their conversation. "What's wrong? What happened?" I asked them.

They didn't respond. They just gave me annoyed, quizzical looks. They seemed offended that I, a person with neither a green smock nor a stethoscope hanging around my neck, would interrupt a serious medical conference.

"Can I go in?" I asked, indicating the door to Bill's room. Again, I got no response, just those blank stares. I took that as permission and barged into the room.

Bill looked fine. In fact, he looked better than when I left. Now it was he who was giving me the quizzical stare.

"What happened to you?" I shouted.

"I took a short nap," he said. "What the hell happened to you? You look like you're scared out of your wits."

"There are three doctors outside," I told him.

"This is a hospital. They have a lot of them around here."

"But they're right outside your door. That didn't look good."

"Well, it looks very good to me," he said. "If they were inside my door all three of them would be sending me a bill by tomorrow morning."

I felt dumb, but still my fear was justified. "I thought there might be a problem."

Bill said, "I'm fine."

"You're not fine," I said. "You're in a hospital. Something is wrong. Tell me what it is."

"I told you. It's Antimacassar Syndrome."

"Yeah. I know you told me that's what you have. I looked it up in a medical dictionary."

"And?"

"It wasn't there," I said.

"See, I told you it was rare. The medical books don't even know about it."

"So I looked it up in a regular dictionary. An antimacassar is a doily that's thrown over the back of a chair to protect it from hair pomade."

"Yeah, but did they also mention that there's no known cure for it?"

"Bill, look, something's wrong with you and I care about you. If you don't want to tell me what the problem is, that's fine. But when I saw those doctors outside your room, I thought there might have been an emergency or something."

Bill told me, "Well, there was kind of an emergency in here."

"I knew it," I said. "What happened?"

"I was stuck in this room for about a half an hour with no hoagie."

"I don't know what sort of disease you have, but I know this—your sick brain is incurable." I put the brown paper bag with the hoagies in it on the night table next to his bed.

He let it sit there. That wasn't a good sign. Normally, Bill would have lunged at the food and began his lesson with a mouth full of delicious Philly fare.

"Aren't you going to eat?" I asked. "I thought you were starving."

"I am," he said. "But first I want to get our final lesson out of the way."

"What final lesson?"

"As I told you earlier, you're about ready to take your final exam. You're nearing graduation. But I have one final lesson before you get your diploma."

"Bill, we don't have to do this now . . ."

"Yes we do. It's important to me. And for you. This lesson will change your life. It can change anyone's life."

"Wow," I said. "If it's that important, I sure want to learn it."

Bill asked, "What is it that you most want to achieve?"

"You know what it is."

"I want you to tell me."

"I want to be a successful stand-up comedian."

"Okay. I'm going to turn you into a successful stand-up comedian."

"Well, you've been doing a pretty good job of it so far."

"No, I mean tonight. Right now."

"Right now? This minute?"

"Exactly."

"Is this going to make me a successful stand-up comedian the way it made you a guardian angel?"

Bill said, "I'm serious about this, Chuck."

Again, there's no arguing with Bill Shaugnessy, AKA Archangel Shecky. I said, "Okay, make me a star."

"Repeat after me. I am a successful stand-up comedian."

I did. I said, "I am a successful stand-up comedian."

Bill said, "Okay, that's it."

"That's it?"

"That's it."

"When does my fan club show up?"

"That may take a little while."

"Bill, you're playing games with me."

He pointed his finger at me, which he liked to do when he was getting very serious. "I definitely am not playing games with you. This is the most important lesson you'll learn from me. In fact, it's the most important lesson you'll learn in your whole life."

"Well, I'm not making light of it. I just don't know quite what the lesson is yet."

Bill was going to tell me. "The first link in the chain of events that will lead anyone to accomplish whatever they want is to believe and to know that you have already achieved it. In your case, you are a successful stand-up comedian."

I wasn't buying it. "Bill, I'm sorry, but this all sounds like hocus-pocus, malarkey, baloney, hogwash, nonsense, and whatever other names there are for it."

Bill ignored my objections like always. "Some people claim you have to want something in your heart. They're wrong. There's a big difference between wanting something and having something. When you have it, you have it. When you want something, you don't have it. By definition, you don't have it. If you had it, you wouldn't want it. Does that make sense?"

"Maybe on the way home it will."

"When you believe—when you know—that you have what you want, good things start to happen."

"Bill," I objected again, "If I tell myself that, I'll feel like I'm lying to myself."

"Well, we've established two things since I came into this hospital—I'm no longer an angel, but you're still a nitwit."

"How can I convince myself that I'm a successful stand-up comedian when I'm not yet a successful stand-up comedian?"

"Let me explain it to you this way. Suppose I give you a bunch of flower seeds—name some flowers."

"What?"

"C'mon, humor me. I'm sick. Name some flowers."

"Pansies, petunias, snapdragons . . ."

"Good, you went for ones with funny names. That's good. Okay, now, suppose I give you some packets of seeds for those pansies, snapdragons, and whatever else you said. And you plant them in the ground. Okay?"

I went along with him. "Okay."

"What have you just done?"

"I planted pansies, petunias, and snapdragons."

"There's nothing there. All you've got in front of you is dirt. Yet, you're telling me that you planted pansies, petunias, and snapdragons. Is that lying?"

"No. They've got to grow."

"So does whatever you want to achieve. It has to grow. But you still believe that you planted those flowers. And some day, there are going to be beautiful flowers where now there is just dirt."

"I'm not sure those examples are quite the same."

"When legendary performers like Sinatra, Presley, Judy Garland used to come onto a stage, they strutted onto that stage strong and proud—like they owned it."

I said, "Sure they did, but that's Frank and Elvis and Judy."

Bill acted as if I had just made his point for him. "So? They weren't always superstars. Do you think they walked onstage like little nebbishes until they were a big hit and then they started walking proud?"

"No, I guess not," I admitted.

"Of course not. They believed they were somebodies even when they were nobodies. You have to know and believe that you are what you want to be now and then allow the rest of the world to catch up to you."

"I don't know, Bill," I said. I was just being honest with him.

"I know it sounds like malarkey, poppycock, baloney, and whatever else you called it earlier. And that's good."

"Why is that good?"

"Because it keeps a lot of people from trying it. That makes it easier for those of us—you and me, for example—who believe it works. And I'll tell you why it works."

"You must have had a good nap. Class is going overtime tonight."

"We're winding up the school year, we have to complete the curriculum. Here's why your belief works. When somebody believes they already are what they want to be, they begin to think, act, and work like what they want to become. You want to be a comedian. If you honestly believe you are, you'll write like a pro, you'll do whatever a pro would do. That belief affects all of your actions. Your actions then help lead to your achievement."

"That's starting to make more sense to me."

"Your solid belief in yourself affects how others view you, too. If you look and act and perform like a professional, people will look on you as a professional. Not only the audiences you perform in front of, but also the bookers, the agents, the producers—the whole shebang."

"That's pretty powerful."

"I warned you. Your belief right now will affect how you view yourself. You'll be more confident, more upbeat, you'll want to walk onstage right now the way Frank, Elvis, and Judy attacked the stage."

Somewhere in the dark recesses of my mind a light went on. I was beginning to get it. "This is really powerful stuff."

"It will affect how you view others in relationship to yourself. You'll bring a powerful force to all your dealings with others."

"You're offering some pretty strong sales points."

"It's not that I'm such a dynamic salesman; it's that I have a good product. See, most of us think backwards. We say something like, 'If I could just get a job writing on the *Tonight Show*, then I'd write terrific jokes, then I'd be recognized as a great comedy writer.' It happens in other areas, too. Some folks say 'If they would make me the supervisor of this department, I'd work real hard and do a good job as supervisor, then the bosses would make me a real executive.'"

"What's wrong with that?"

"I already told you—it's backwards. It's 'Have-Do-Be' thinking."

"What's that?" I asked.

"It means a person wants to get something first—to have it. Then he would do the work required. Then he would be what he wants to be."

"And your suggestion is?"

"Let me ask you this. Let's go back to our friend and prime example, Tiger Woods. Suppose he said, 'If only I could play in the Masters, then I'd learn to hit the golf ball really well, then I'd be a great golfer.' Does that make sense to you?"

"Not when you put it that way."

"Of course not. Tiger first had to be a good golfer, then he would do what great golfers do. Only then could he win the Masters and be recognized as a great golfer. That's the do part. Then he could have the prestige and the money and the respect that he earned. He had to use the 'Be-Do-Have' philosophy."

"So you're saying you have to be great first, then you can do great things, then you can be recognized as great."

Bill was delighted. "A-plus for you in this class. You have to be whatever it is you want to be, even if it's only in your own head or your own estimation. Then you'll do those things that will make you excel in whatever it is you want to be. Then you'll have whatever it is you were shooting for. Just like those little seeds you planted in the ground knew that they were pansies, petunias, and snapdragons, you have to know that you are whatever it is you want to be."

"Well, I disagree with you."

"You don't accept that philosophy?"

"No, I disagree when you said you weren't a dynamic salesman. You've sold me on that concept. It makes sense."

"Good, because that's your assignment for tonight and for the rest of your career—believe in yourself. Know that you've got whatever it takes to achieve whatever you want.

"And finally—class dismissed. Here's your diploma." He handed me a napkin that he must have written while I was on my hoagie run. It must have been important because it was underlined. It read:

Be whatever you want to be—Right Now

I said, "Thanks, Bill. This really means a lot to me."

He said, "It'll mean more as the years go by." Now that class was over, he got back to the reason I came here in the first place.

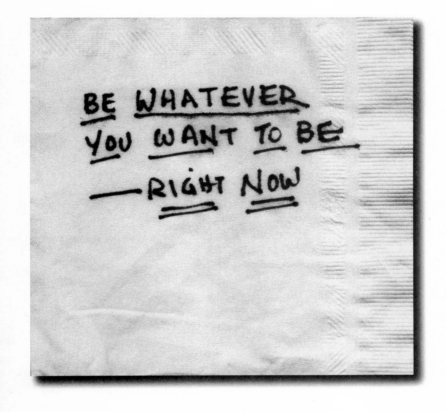

He said, "Now let's talk about your dilemma. On this cruise, you'll be working almost every night, which is great experience. You'll be working with an audience that really wants to have fun. They'll be very receptive. You'll have plenty of time on the cruise to do some writing. That is if you decide to work and not just sit on your ass by the pool with a fancy drink with an umbrella in it. It's a good opportunity."

I added, "I think so, too."

"However, it's a gamble. You're giving up your income. Meager as it likely is. You'll be committing yourself to comedy whether you like it or not. And you'll be working without a net."

"That's right."

"You've asked me to make a decision and I've made my decision."

I was eager to hear his advice.

"My decision," he began, "is that I'm not going to make a decision."

"But, Bill," I said, "You've always been such a help to me..."

"This is your life, your gamble, your career. You'll get the rewards or you'll suffer the consequences. It would be inappropriate, it would be wrong for me to make this decision for you. If I made it for you now, you'd just have to make it for yourself later on. This is your moment; you have to live with it."

"Well, if I take the job, do you think I'll be doing the right thing?"

"What I think doesn't matter. And whether you'll be doing the right thing or not doesn't matter, either."

Now he had me totally confused. "What do you mean it doesn't matter? This could make or break me."

"Not really. It could make you, but it won't break you."

"Bill, how can you say that?"

"Because it's true. If it's the right thing, your career picks up speed. If it's the wrong thing, you drop it and work hard to find the right thing. No wrong decision is irreversible."

"But I thought you could at least help me with . . ."

"Remember we talked earlier. In fact, I gave you a napkin on it and you agreed to it. That little piece of advice: Whatever happens, good or bad, is your responsibility. You decide."

"But, Bill, there's another thing. I'd have to leave almost immediately. I hate to go away while you're in the hospital."

Bill said emphatically, "It's your responsibility. Kid, stop worrying about me. If you decide to take this gig, worry about your act on those cruises. Write great material and try it out on those audiences. That's where your head should be right now. Me? I'll be here when you get back."

"Is that a promise?"

"Have I ever lied to you before?"

"Let's see. You said you were my guardian angel. You said you had never tasted a cheese steak, had never heard of scrapple, never bit into a Tastykake . . ."

"All right, I withdraw the question. But as your mentor, as your former guardian angel, as a person who knows all things, as your friend, I'm telling you I'll be here when you get back."

We were both silent for a moment.

"You'd better get started," he said.

"I guess so."

I started to leave, but turned back at the door. "I may not see you again for four to six weeks or more."

"I know."

I still wanted reassurance. "You promise you'll be here when I get back?"

He gave me a thumbs up sign and said, "Hey, if you can't trust your guardian angel, who can you trust? I'll be here."

CHAPTER EIGHTEEN...

HE WASN'T.

After my Wednesday visit with him at the hospital, I called the next day to tell him that I was going to take that cruise line gig. He was pleased and wished me luck, but things were so frantic that I didn't get a chance to get to the hospital again. By the time I got back from my tour, Bill was gone.

Sally, one of the nurses at St. Agnes's who had cared for Bill told me the usual—it was peaceful, he didn't suffer, he was ready, it was probably a blessing in the long run—all that stuff that means nothing, really. It didn't help ease the hurt, the emptiness, the guilt.

She told me that Bill left no personal belongings except for a letter, sealed and addressed to me.

CHAPTER NINETEEN...

Dear Chuck,

Well, I lied to you once again. I knew I wouldn't be here when you got back. The doctors pretty much assured me of that. They didn't really have to, though. I kind of sensed it for myself. They say that elephants know when it's time for them to die. I'm at least as smart as a pachyderm—a few of them, anyway.

Don't be angry with the doctors or the hospital staff. I asked them to keep my medical condition totally confidential. I thought it would be better this way. I hate long good-byes. I hate short good-byes, too—especially when I'm the one that's being good-byed.

Congratulations to you. You've graduated from the "Archangel Shecky School of Comedy and Get What You Want-iveness." Even though you finished at the top of your graduating class of one, I've appointed myself valedictorian. Since you were at the top of your class, maybe you think you should have been given that honor. However, it's my school, so I'm the valedictorian. If you want to be a valedictorian, start your own school.

I'm not going to try to teach you any more about comedy writing because now that you've thrown yourself into the business full time, you've got the greatest comedy teacher in the world— your audience. Respect them, listen to them, learn from them and you'll get yourself a Ph.D. in comedy.

I'll just remind you to keep writing to a quota. That'll keep your writing muscle limber and your act fresh.

However, as a graduate of Archangel Shecky's School of Comedy and Get What You Want-iveness, one of the duties you owe to your Alma Mater is to help others in their own pursuit. Here are a few of the things that I tried to help you with and that I hope you'll help others with. These principles are not limited to comedy writing; they apply regardless of the goal a person wants to achieve.

Of course, if you want to achieve a goal, you first have to decide on what that goal is. The key word in that advice is "you." This should be your goal—not what tradition or society tells you is your pre-ordained destiny. It's not what your parents or friends decide for you. It should be your dream.

Once you determine your goal, here is a numbered list of other items your students should remember:

1. If you want to be great, start with "lousy." Just get started. You can't "get better" until you take that first step. Usually that first step is downright awful, but it has to be there so you can improve on it. Remember, there's nothing wrong with being lousy. The problem is in staying lousy or giving up entirely.

2. You deserve whatever it is you want. Don't make the mistake of abandoning a dream because you consider yourself unworthy of it. You have as much right to whatever it is you want as anyone else in the world. You have the right to go after it with all the gusto you can muster.

3. You already know how to be a success. It's very easy to say, "I can't do this" or "I can't do that," but the reality is that

you can do it or you can learn to do it. Think of all the skills you've achieved . . . all that you've accomplished. Even the most trivial of your achievements—like learning to walk and drive—have taught you how to be successful. Remember the steps you took with them, and apply them to your present pursuit.

4. *Persevere.* Keep going until you get it. No matter what you're trying to achieve, you're going to get kicked in the teeth from time to time. You'll experience disappointments, setbacks, heartbreaks. Allow yourself a period of self-pity or "why me-ism" if you like, but only a short one. Then buck up and return to your pursuit. Winston Churchill said, "*Success consists of going from failure to failure without loss of enthusiasm.*"

5. You must believe—you must know—that you can achieve what you want. Belief in yourself and your talent is an important stimulus to achievement. You must generate confidence even to the point of absolutely knowing that you have what it takes to accomplish your goal. Henry Ford once said, "*If you think you can do a thing or think you can't do a thing, you're right.*"

6. *You must be willing to pay the price.* Every worthwhile goal has a price tag attached to it. Once you agree to pay that price, you must keep on making the payments. You must do whatever it is you have to do to ensure your success. Sometimes these payments can be surprisingly steep. Keep your goal in view and remember that "*you get what you pay for.*"

7. Whatever happens to you—good or bad—is your responsibility. No whining, complaining, or blaming other people or circumstances. You must deal with all obstacles, whether they're fair or

unfair. Either turn them to your advantage, overcome them, or find a way around them. It's often tempting and much too easy to blame other people or circumstances for your problems. But whatever the cause, they become your problems. You are obliged to deal with them. You must accept total responsibility.

8. _Be good at what you do and keep getting better._ I've underlined this chunk of advice (just as I did when I wrote it on a napkin for you). Bottom line, this is the secret to success—in anything. This is the formula that everything else is based on. If you are good at whatever you do and you keep getting better and better at it, eventually you'll arrive at excellence. Excellence, in any field, can't be denied; it must be noticed . . . and rewarded.

9. Always continue to learn. In order to do what you want to do, you must know what you're doing. Knowledge in any endeavor is power. An interesting phenomenon about learning is that the more you learn, the more you realize how much more you have to learn. Get as much knowledge as you can from as many different sources as you can. It will pay off in your quest.

10. Practice, practice, practice. Even if you know where you're going and you know how to get there, you still must be certain that you have the skills, the techniques, and the drive that will get you there. Devotion to your craft—practice, practice, practice—gives you that assurance.

11. Hone your technique. Even after you learn the basic skills, you can still improve. You add your own style, your own flair, your own innovations. When you do that, you become a standout in your field. You become an expert who can't be overlooked.

12. *Prepare ahead*—have a plan of action . . . broken into bite-sized chunks. *Study, research, investigate.* Find out as much about your particular goal and what is necessary to reach it as you can. Then use this information to design a plan for pursuing your dream. The plan can be detailed or loosely structured. One way or another, though, know where you are, where you're going, and how you're going to get there. Avoid trying to "eat the whole steak in one mouthful." Be patient and content with incremental progress. Plan to move from Point A to Point B, then from Point B to Point C and so on. Success, they say, is a journey. Enjoy each part of the trip.

13. *Be prepared for setbacks.* Develop a failure-is-not-an-option attitude. During your journey you will meet with obstacles. Your research will help you here. You should have learned of some of the pitfalls between you and your goal. Expect them. Prepare for them. If you know they're coming, you can have the necessary mind-set to deal with them. Recognize that obstacles are challenges, not failure.

14. <u>Be a success right now</u>. (Again, I've underlined this point. It's that important.) Believe in your own head that you are the person you wish to become—that you've already achieved whatever goal you seek. Think, act, and perform as that successful person. Others will see you that way and react accordingly. It's applying the Be-Do-Have principle to your quest. Be the person you want to be. That will enable you to do what that person would do. Then you'll have all the rewards that person would enjoy.

Now, Chuck, we have to discuss your tuition. That's right, you still have a student loan to settle. You should know by now that nothing you do with me is free. Don't fret, though. You'll be able to afford it.

You'll do well with your comedy; I know you will. Someday, somebody may need a little boost, encouragement, and maybe some education—just like you did. When you meet that person, or those people, be generous. Help them to help themselves. When you do that, I'll consider your student loan paid in full. Who knows, maybe someday you can be somebody's guardian angel.

I envy you, Chuck, and the others you're going to mentor along the way. All of you are on an exciting journey. The destination is important, but remember to have fun along the way. Enjoy your adventure. You'll probably discover when you reach your pinnacle that the advertising slogan was right—'Getting there is half the fun.'

Keep working at your craft, Chuck. Keep getting better. And maybe think of me once in awhile.

Your good friend and guardian angel,
Archangel Shecky (AKA Bill Shaughnessy)

CHAPTER TWENTY...

A FEW WEEKS LATER, A LAWYER NAMED BRETT MICHAELSON called and asked if I could stop by his office whenever it was convenient. In his will, William Shaughnessy bequeathed to one Charles Barry—that was me—the sum of $364.86.

In the documentation that accompanied the check, every scotch, cheese steak, milk shake, Tastykake, soft pretzel, hoagie, and cup of coffee was itemized. Bill, through his will, reimbursed me for every single one, including tax and a generous tip. He even picked up my tab for a few of them.

Why Bill tricked me into footing the bill for everything while he was alive, I don't know. Maybe he thought that if I was investing my own money, I'd pay more attention to what he was saying. He may have been right about that.

Anyway, he repaid every cent. Bill Shaughnessy may not have been an angel, but he wasn't a deadbeat, either.

EPILOGUE...

"HERE'S THE BLACK COFFEE YOU WANTED, MR. BARRY. IS IT hot enough for you?" She asked.

I sipped it and it was delicious and threateningly hot. Even the aroma revitalized me after an exhausting, stressful but successful first show. "It's perfect," I said.

I tipped the cocktail waitress generously. Reaching the stage where I was required to tip generously was all right with me.

She said, "Thank you. That was a great show tonight, Mr. Barry. Congratulations."

"I appreciate that," I said.

"Is there anything else I can get for you?"

I said, "No, thank you. Just close the door when you leave and tell them that I don't want any visitors between shows—nobody at all."

"Will do," she said as she left.

I wasn't being cocky, arrogant, or big headed. I just wanted some time alone to savor this night. My career had been going well for some time now. Things started to turn around with those gigs on the cruise lines. I scored well on those first few trips and that got me plenty more cruise gigs. That allowed me to work much more than I would have otherwise.

That many comedy shows demanded lots of new material so I wrote and tried out plenty of jokes and built up my comedy repertoire quickly.

The audiences were tremendously receptive. That helped me build up my confidence, develop my stage persona, and find my comedy voice.

The cruises were terrific exposure, too. Many influential people watched me perform on the ships, appreciated my style, and helped me find many impressive bookings—on land.

Don't get me wrong, though. It wasn't a perfectly smooth ride from there to here. I got kicked in the teeth plenty of times, just like Bill warned I would. There were times of doubt, depression—sometimes something close to despair. But that's when I leaned on that mantra Bill drummed into me: "I am a successful stand-up comedian." I'd force myself to believe it was true. That belief prompted me to think the way a successful stand-up comedian would think and to act the way a successful stand-up comedian would act.

I couldn't forget that Archangel Shecky's—good heavens, it's been a long time since I've used that phrase—that Archangel Shecky's secret of success was to be good at what you do and keep getting better. Rather than waste time feeling sorry for myself that things weren't going as well I wanted them to or moving as quickly as I would have liked, I'd work on something that would make me or my act a little bit better. Damned if it didn't work.

Comedy clubs, not only in Philly but across the country, were now booking me steadily as a headliner at a pretty good salary. Eight guest appearances on the *Tonight Show*—

where I scored better and better each time—gave a tremendous boost to my career.

My agent feels pretty strongly that NBC is going to have me starring in my own sitcom either this year or next. In fact, there are strong rumors that I could be the leading contender to take over the *Tonight Show* desk if that spot ever opens up.

But tonight was special. I had just done my first show as the featured attraction in the big room at the MGM Grand in Las Vegas. It went well and I just wanted a private moment to let all of it soak in. After the second show I'd have a lot of friends and celebrities visiting me in my dressing room, but right now I preferred to be alone.

"That was a helluva show you did tonight," someone said from behind me.

"What?" I turned and there was a man who looked like a mobster. He was dressed in gaudy, well-tailored, expensive clothes like Robert DeNiro in *Casino*.

I said, "What the hell are you doing in here? This is my private dressing room."

"I belong in here," he replied.

I shouted, "The only people who belong in here are the ones I say belong in here. Now get the hell out. I'm calling security."

I picked up the phone but something stopped me, "Who the hell are you anyway?"

"I'm your guardian angel."

I slammed the phone down. I could call security anytime and they'd be there in a flash—they were just outside the door—but first I had something I wanted to say to this little pissant. I pointed my finger at him and said, "Look, pal, I don't know who you are or where you came from. I don't know how you got in here. And I don't know what you heard about my good friend Bill and me. But don't you ever play games with it. Bill was a great guy and I owe everything I have to him. So you just keep your mouth shut about Bill, do you understand?"

He said, "I do understand and I agree with you. Bill is a great guy and you do owe a lot to him."

"Damn right. So before I call security and have them throw your sorry ass out of here, who the hell are you really?"

"I'm your real guardian angel," he said. "Always have been."

That did it. I punched the security code on the phone, "Get Jimmy in here...fast," I said to whoever it was who answered. Jimmy was the head of my personal security here at the MGM Grand and he was one tough sonofagun.

The intruder said, "Why don't you have a taste of your coffee while you're waiting?"

I said, "Don't worry, pal, it won't be a long wait." Then I did sip from my coffee cup and spit it out almost immediately.

"What the hell?" I said. "This is wine."

He said, "Yeah, I know. Bill said you'd get a kick out of that one."

There was a loud knock on my dressing room door and Jimmy hollered in, "Did you call for me, Mr. Barry?"

I didn't quite know what to think, but I needed time. I answered, "Yeah, Jimmy. Just give me a second, will you. Everything's all right."

He hollered, "Are you sure?"

I said, "Yeah, I'm fine." Then I said to the DeNiro dress-alike, "Is this some kind of trick? A practical joke or something? I know what it is. You're from the magic show over at the Monte Carlo. Right?"

He said, "No trick. I really am your guardian angel. I'm the guy who helped you avoid that accident outside of Rohn's drug store."

"How did you know about that?"

"I was there. I made you miss your turn. That's what we guardian angels do."

"Yeah, well how about the guy who was in the accident there. What happened to his guardian angel?"

The guy shrugged. "I don't know. Maybe he just had an off day."

I said, "Look, I can't go through this again. I'm doing well now, I don't need a guardian angel hanging around."

"Pal, you're big time show biz. You need a guardian angel more now than you ever did. But I won't be hanging around—not in this form anyway. This is a special, one-time-only deal. I'll be around—always—but you won't be seeing me again."

Jimmy hollered from outside my dressing room door again. "Are you sure you're all right in there, Mr. Barry?"

I said, "I'm just fine, Jimmy. I'm in good hands."

My guardian angel said, "Damn right you are."

"You know this is a little hard to take," I said. "I had enough trouble with it with Bill, when it was all a game, but this..." I took another sip of my coffee-merlot. It was soft with a good balance of tannin and just the right amount of oak. My guardian winemaker knew his stuff.

Then it dawned on me. Bill had been gone for years. Why was I now getting this visit? "What are you doing here?" I asked.

"I'm here on a special mission."

"What?"

"You'll find out."

There was a knock on the door. I hollered, "It's okay, Jimmy. I'm fine."

A voice outside the door answered, "It's Jeannie. I've got some new lines for you to look at."

"Okay, Jeannie. Give me a minute." I motioned towards the door and said to. . . I guess, my guardian angel, "I'm sorry, but you'd better deliver your message now. That's my writer and we've got some work to do before the next show."

"You write new material between shows?"

I explained, "Yeah. I do a bit where I read headlines from today's paper and then do some adlibs about them. My writer, Jeannie, does most of the adlibs for me."

"You read from the headlines? Will Rogers used to do that bit almost 100 years ago, didn't he?"

"Yeah, he did. Bill taught me to respect and study the old timers. It works."

"I'm sure it does."

"Yeah, well, I will have to ask you to excuse us because we do have some work to do."

Jeannie knocked on the door again—harder this time. "Chuck, we don't have much time to go over these lines."

Guardian angels must all be stubborn. He said, "I really would like to stay."

"Suit yourself," I said. "But we'll be busy."

"I won't interrupt."

Jeannie charged through the door when I opened it, went right to the couch and spread some pages out on the coffee table. She read me the lines she had just written. I asked her a few questions about several of them, and suggested word changes in a few. She penciled my edits into the margin of her typed pages.

Then I read over the revised lines again and put a large X in the margin of those gags I liked and wanted to do for the next performance.

"Don't you want to include this one?" Jeannie asked, indicating one of the gags I hadn't checked.

"No," I said, "I don't like it."

"It's a great joke," Jeannie said. "The audience will love it."

"Really?"

"Absolutely," she said.

I tore that single joke from the page, handed it to her and said, "Then here. Put it in your act."

She crumpled the paper up and tossed it aside. "You son of a ...."

"Jeannie," I interrupted her before she cursed in front of an honest to God angel, "get these new lines typed up and put them inside the newspaper for the next show."

Before she could leave, my guardian angel, who had dutifully remained unobtrusive during our brief conference, stepped toward her extending his hand.

He said, "Hello, Jeannie."

Jeannie said, "Hi," having no idea who she was greeting. As she shook his hand, she said, "Jeannie Casilli."

I felt I had to formally introduce them now. "This is my head-writer, Jeannie. We connected back in Philly, we worked together for awhile and now she handles most of the writing for my act. And she's brilliant."

Jeannie said, "I wasn't brilliant at first. Not until Chuck taught me everything I know."

"Yeah, but you did the work" the angel said to Jeannie, sounding a lot like Bill used to.

I continued the introduction. "Jeannie this is...." I had no idea what his name was and was not about to introduce him as "my guardian angel."

He rescued me. "I'm Wilton, Jeannie. It's very nice to meet you."

Jeannie said, "Nice to meet you."

The angel said, "So Chuck was your mentor in comedy?"

"Right," she answered with a nod toward me.

The angel said, "He was kind of like your comedy guardian angel."

"I don't know if I'd go that far," she laughed. "I rarely use the words 'Chuck' and 'angel' in the same sentence." She quickly added, "Look, it's nice to meet you, but I've got to run." She waved the script pages to indicate she had to get them typed and put into the prop newspaper.

Before she could dash out the angel quickly asked, "Are you married, Jeannie?"

She looked bothered by that strange question from a relative stranger, but said, "Yes, I am."

I started to wonder if I had a guardian angel who was hitting on my head-writer.

He asked, "What was your name before you were married?"

She said, "Shaughnessy, but I really have to run."

She exited quickly.

I just stared at him, stunned.

I stammered, "Is she....."

"Yes. That's Bill's granddaughter. The one he never met—he never even knew her name."

"Wow," was all I could manage to say. I held up my coffee cup. "Can you turn this coffee into anything stronger?"

"Sorry," he said, "We don't deal in hard liquor."

"She has no idea who Bill Shaughnessy was?"

"That's right. She has no idea who Bill Shaughnessy is . . . or that she's his granddaughter. And she has no need to know."

"Of course not," I agreed. "But isn't it an unbelievable coincidence that I would . . ."

"Not really," my guardian angel said. "In my line of work there are no coincidences."

I asked, "Was that your mission? The message you had to deliver?"

He nodded. "Bill got special permission for me to come here. He wanted to thank you and to let you know that your tuition is all paid up."

"This is really incredible."

My guardian angel answered a bit smugly, "Not really. We deal in the incredible. It is unusual, though. In fact, almost unheard of, but then it seemed very important to Bill."

"And Bill can be a very persuasive guy."

He said, "God only knows."

"I'm honest to goodness flabbergasted," I confessed. "Can I ask you something, though?"

"Sure."

"Why didn't Bill come himself?"

"We thought about that, but the Big Boss felt that the expense account would be prohibitive."

I said, "I know what He means."

Then Wilton said, "I really should get back now."

"You know, Bill used to write his advice to me on napkins all the time."

"Of course I know that. I was there."

"I thought it was silly at the time. Don't ask me why, but for some reason I saved every one of those napkins. I had them all put in one frame and have them hanging in my office."

He said, "I know."

"I call them my Sheckyisms."

"That's nice."

"Whenever things aren't going just right for me, I read them over. It always helps me. They really work, you know."

"Yes, they do."

I said, "I wish Bill could see them."

"He has. He loves the frame."

"Thanks for saying that. It means a lot to me."

"I really should be going now," he said.

I didn't want him to leave. I said, "Can I get you something before you go?"

He said, "No, thanks, I really . . . well, you know, maybe I'll try a taste of that scotch that Bill raves about."

I went to the bar set up in my dressing room, dropped a few ice cubes in a glass, poured some scotch, handed it to him and said, "Cheers."

He took a swallow, opened his eyes wide, and started to choke. He gasped for air, and then choked again.

I pounded him on the back and offered him water. He ignored everything I was doing or saying and just continued to alternately choke and gasp for breath.

Finally, he recovered enough to speak. Brushing back tears from his eyes caused by the choking, he said, "Boy, this stuff is damned good. No wonder Bill loves it."

I just laughed.

He laughed along with me and said, "I really have to go now."

I said, "Yeah, well, okay. What do you do? Do you go out the door? Do you disappear in a puff of smoke? What?"

He said, "I'll show myself out."

I quickly added, "Are you sure you wouldn't like to stay and see the next show?"

"No, thank you. I couldn't be seen in public dressed like this."

I laughed again. He had a good sense of humor for an angel—especially an angel named Wilton.

He went to the door and reached for the handle, but I couldn't let him leave without asking, "Bill, is he...uh..."

"Bill's fine," he said. "He's with us now and he's very proud of you. He says to call on him anytime you need anything."

"Tell him I'll do that."

"Oh, one more thing. Bill said to tell you he's very happy in Heaven, but the food in Philly is much better."